"I'm Scared Of How Far Out Of My Depth I Am."

The words tumbled out in a breathy rush. "I don't know what you want from me."

"I think you do know. I think that's what scares you."

Nick's voice was as soft as the moonlight. T.C. felt a shiver run through her. Not cold, but heat. "Casual sex isn't something I handle well," she breathed.

"You think this would be casual?"

Her startled gaze flew to his and was immediately trapped by his intent expression. Her breathing grew shallow; her pulse pounded like racing hoofbeats on summer-hard earth.

"I imagine nothing's ever casual with you," he said slowly.

Dear Reader,

Welcome to Silhouette Desire! We're delighted to offer you again this month six passionate, powerful and provocative romances sure to please you.

Start with December's fabulous MAN OF THE MONTH, *A Cowboy's Promise*. This latest title in Anne McAllister's popular CODE OF THE WEST miniseries features a rugged Native American determined to win back the woman he left three years before. Then discover *The Secret Life of Connor Monahan* in Elizabeth Bevarly's tale of a vice cop who mistakenly surmises that a prim and proper restaurateur is operating a call-girl ring.

The sizzling miniseries 20 AMBER COURT concludes with Anne Marie Winston's *Risqué Business*, in which a loyal employee tries to prevent a powerful CEO with revenge on his mind from taking over the company she thinks of as her family. Reader favorite Maureen Child delivers the next installment of another exciting miniseries, THE FORTUNES OF TEXAS: THE LOST HEIRS. In *Did You Say Twins?!* a marine sergeant inherits twin daughters and is forced to turn for help to the woman who refused his marriage proposal ten years before.

The sexy hero of *Michael's Temptation,* the last book in Eileen Wilks's TALL, DARK & ELIGIBLE miniseries, goes to Central America to rescue a lovely lady who's been captured by guerrillas. And sparks fly when a smooth charmer and a sassy tomboy are brought together by their shared inheritance of an Australian horse farm in Brownyn Jameson's *Addicted to Nick*.

Take time out from the holiday rush and treat yourself to all six of these not-to-be-missed romances.

Enjoy,

Joan Marlow Golan

Joan Marlow Golan
Senior Editor, Silhouette Desire

Please address questions and book requests to:
Silhouette Reader Service
U.S.: 3010 Walden Ave., P.O. Box 1325, Buffalo, NY 14269
Canadian: P.O. Box 609, Fort Erie, Ont. L2A 5X3

Addicted to Nick
BRONWYN JAMESON

Silhouette Desire

Published by Silhouette Books
America's Publisher of Contemporary Romance

SILHOUETTE BOOKS

ISBN 0-373-76410-3

ADDICTED TO NICK

Visit Silhouette at www.eHarlequin.com

Printed in U.S.A.

Books by Bronwyn Jameson

Silhouette Desire

In Bed with the Boss's Daughter #1380
Addicted to Nick #1410

BRONWYN JAMESON

spent much of her childhood with her head buried in a book. As a teenager, she discovered romance novels, and it was only a matter of time before she turned her love of reading them into a love of writing them. Bronwyn shares an idyllic piece of the Australian farming heartland with her husband and three sons, a thousand sheep, a dozen horses, assorted wildlife and one kelpie dog. She still chooses to spend her limited downtime with a good book. Bronwyn loves to hear from readers. Write to her at bronwyn@bronwynjameson.com.

Prologue

Nick didn't know what coming home should feel like, but he figured something ought to register on the nostalgia scale. Nothing major, mind you, just a touch of the warm and fuzzies. Hell, even a twinge of bitterness would be better than the emotional numbness that seemed to have settled over him during the long flight from JFK to Australia.

He hated the lack of feeling. It reminded him too keenly of the first time he'd stood in this drive gazing up at Joe Corelli's mansion, except that time he had deliberately schooled his eight-year-old heart to blankness. He hadn't wanted to feel anything—not fear or confusion, shame or hope—so he'd simply looked at the big house and wondered how long till someone realized they'd made a serious mistake.

Kids like Niccolo Corelli got arrested for being anywhere near houses like this.

But the stranger who introduced himself as some rela-

tive of his dead mother had looped a comforting arm
around his shoulders and said, "This is your home, Niccolo. Forget what came before—you're part of my family
now."

Part of a family.

Nick hadn't a clue what that meant, and, despite Joe's
best efforts, he'd never been allowed to forget his origins.

He stared a while longer at the big house and felt nothing. Maybe he just needed sleep. Ten hours, uninterrupted,
between sheets. Yeah, that was exactly what his jet-lagged
body and emotion-lagged mind needed, although they
weren't getting horizontal yet. With a barely stifled yawn,
he unfolded himself from the hire car and stretched his
limbs. Then, as he turned toward the house, he caught a
flicker of movement at an upstairs window.

Big Brother George watching from on high.

Just like that first time, Nick thought, although today he
raised a casual hand in acknowledgment instead of the
single-finger salute of fourteen years before. The curtain
shifted back into place, and Nick puffed out a derisive
laugh. Idly he scanned the ground-floor windows and wondered who else might be watching.

How many of the four women who had grown up as his
sisters waited inside the thick stucco walls? Sophie, no
doubt. At the faintest whiff of trouble, Sophie always came
running. She was the one who dobbed to her mother the
first time he bloodied George's nose...and to her father the
last time. It was Sophie who eavesdropped on the heated
argument between her parents before Joe brought him here,
and who spread the phrase "dirty whore's brat."

Yeah, he would bet money on Sophie turning up—if
George had bothered to let his sisters know he was coming.
His adoptive brother's communication record was some-
thing less than stellar.

He slammed the car door on that thought, but as he
strode up the drive, he could feel the tension in his jaw

and a stiffness in his muscles that had nothing to do with jet lag. He didn't want to be here—not here in Melbourne, nor at the country stables he had reportedly inherited.

Reportedly.

Wasn't it just like George to play petty games with the facts and to ensure that the solicitor handling Joe's estate played along, too? Nick blew out an exasperated breath. As soon as he learned the full story and slapped a For Sale sign on Yarra Park, he was gone.

This time for good.

One

If the night hadn't been so still, silent but for the occasional swoosh of straw under restless hooves, T.C. wouldn't have heard the faint creak of gate hinges.

Or the crunch of footsteps on the gravel path leading from the house-yard to the stables.

She could have made her way back to the stable hand's quarters at the far end of the barn and crawled back into bed, convinced her sleep had been disturbed by an unfamiliar and unforgiving mattress rather than the audible signs of a midnight intruder.

The footsteps paused, and a chill of fear shivered across her skin. "Turn around and go back the way you came. Get in your car and drive away. Please." Her entreaty was a whisper of breath that barely pierced the thick night air. She closed her eyes, counted to ten—slowly—but no car door clicked shut, no starter-motor engaged. With her heart lurching painfully against her ribs, she edged to the end of the stable row and peered out into the night.

Nothing moved except some ghostly strands of autumn fog—strands that seemed to slither up from the Yarra River to wrap the house in the promise of winter. T.C. retreated a step, drew a long breath. The air was cold enough to sting in her nostrils, but it was also rich with leather and horsehair, sweet molasses and fresh clover hay, familiar bracing aromas that lent strength to her weak knees.

Someone was out there—maybe the jerk who had dialed her number over and over these past weeks, only to hang up without speaking a word. She pictured him standing on the path, head lifted to test the air as his eyes adjusted to the darkness. Most likely a burglar who thought the place would be easy pickings with only a woman in residence, knowledge he could have gleaned in a casual chat with any of the locals in nearby Riddells Crossing.

Her fingers tightened around the gun in her right hand. It weighed next to nothing yet it felt curiously reassuring, considering it was useless. She switched it to her left hand and wiped her damp palm on her thigh...her *pajama-pants-clad* thigh, she amended. A semihysterical giggle bubbled up, and she pressed a hand to her mouth to stifle the sound.

Some scumbag was stalking her stables, and she intended taking him on dressed in oversize flannel pajamas and armed with nothing but a kid's toy cap gun. She would take him while he was rolling around the floor laughing!

The footsteps started again, approaching rapidly this time and without any pretense of stealth. She had no time to consider this, no time to consider anything, no time to plan. A dark figure came through the barn entrance less than a pace away, close enough for her to absorb the soft tang of his aftershave on a swiftly drawn breath.

Close enough to touch, in the ribs, with the toy gun.

"Don't move, mister, and I won't have to shoot you."

The phoney tough-guy line rolled from T.C.'s tongue

without conscious thought. She closed her eyes and grimaced. Had she really said that? With such cool calm strength, when her insides were quivering like half-set Jell-O? The quaver transferred to her legs and started them trembling. She prayed the hand holding her make-believe weapon wouldn't follow suit.

The stranger slowly raised his hands above his head. "Take it easy, sweetheart. Don't do anything stupid."

"*I* have the, um, gun, so *you* should be the one avoiding stupid moves!" T.C. hated herself for that stumbling pause, but before she could do more than wince, she sensed him start to move and jabbed him with the gun. Hard.

"I get the picture. I'm not to move, right?" He eased out the words in a deep, soothing monotone—the exact same voice she used to settle a nervous horse. That gave her pause. Why was he trying to mollify her? *She* wasn't the one creeping about someone else's stables in the dead of night.

"Right," she clipped out, irritated as well as confused. "No...wrong." She circled about him, transferring the gun from his ribs to his back, as she regathered her composure. "I *do* want you to move. I want you to turn, slowly, and put your hands up against the wall."

Surprisingly he complied, although his posture looked way too casual for T.C.'s liking. "You want me to spread 'em?" he asked. A hint of amusement colored the rich depth of his voice.

"That won't be necessary," she replied, absolutely unamused. The guy acted like having a gun—okay, a *toy* gun, but he didn't know that—pointed at his back was more an entertainment than a concern. She needed to assert some authority, but how on earth did she go about doing that? This was not a small man. At least six foot and, unless her night vision was severely impaired, most of it muscle.

Her only advantage was a handful of plastic imitation weaponry.

What if he had a real weapon?

The alarming thought caused her throat to tighten. She had to clear that solid lump of dread before she could ask, "Are you armed?"

"And dangerous?" he mocked.

T.C. cursed herself for expecting to learn anything from such a foolish question. In order to find out she needed to search him…to put her hands on him….

She steeled herself by drawing a deep breath but found the air edged with his disturbingly appealing scent. She let the breath go with a snort. So even bad guys can find their way around a bottle of Calvin Klein, she told herself. So what? Get on with it!

Plunging forward, she patted down his jacket, found two outside pockets and two sets of keys—nothing unusual there. Her hand stilled on the jacket. Not cheap vinyl but real, malleable, high-quality leather, which did strike her as unusual.

What kind of burglar was he?

"There's an inside pocket you'd better check. And one in my shirt."

Obviously a helpful one.

Stung out of immobility, she took another C.K.-imbued breath before sliding her hand inside the jacket. His shirt was incredibly warm and the fabric so fine that she could feel the muted texture of his chest hair against her palm. And beneath that…*holy toledo!* she felt the rippling curves and indents of some exceedingly fine pecs. It was like stroking the finest horseflesh, all supple and deceptively languid, while underneath the slow, steady beat of his heart pumped all that heat into her hand, her blood, her belly.

Stroking?

She pulled her hand back sharply, and a shimmer of

sensation skimmed across her fingertips, settled in her skin. "Static electricity," she muttered, shaking her fingers.

"Pardon?"

"I wasn't speaking to you."

"Then who?"

"None of your business." T.C. spoke through clenched teeth. "I'm going to search your pants now."

"Be my guest."

It was amazing how much amusement he managed to pack into that short statement. Enough to really rile T.C. She prodded him in the ribs with sufficient force to cause him to flinch. Good—maybe now he would show some respect!

His pants were jeans of the close-fitting variety. One rear pocket housed a slim leather wallet; the other contained nothing more than finely hewn muscle. She took a half step back and wiped her palm against her thigh, then scrubbed it harder. Somehow she couldn't erase the imprint from her skin.

She jumped clear off the ground when he drawled, "Don't stop there, sweet hands. There are more pockets around the front."

"I have a better idea. Why don't you just tell me where your weapon's hidden?"

He laughed, a low rich belly-laugh that did strange things to T.C.'s insides. "Why don't you slide that soft little hand around here and find out for yourself?"

Heat blazed into her cheeks. How dare he be so...so... Words failed her. She did the mental equivalent of spluttering and told herself the warmth in her cheeks was not due to his softly purred suggestion. She transferred the gun from left hand to right, stretched her tight tendons finger by finger, and inspected the hand that was indeed little but hadn't been soft for more years than she could remember.

"Don't," she said, her voice as crisp and chill as the

night air, "make the mistake of associating my size with softness."

And with the strength of those words ringing in her ears, she did exactly as he'd asked. She reached around and checked the front pockets of his jeans. Very quickly. Then she slid her hand up and checked the waistband. Neat fit, hard to hide anything there, she noted. She also noted when he drew breath. She could tell by the sudden tautness of his abs beneath her hand.

What she didn't realize was that the breath was taken in preparation.

His turn was quick, as was the hand that dislodged the gun. It clunked against the wall, hit the floor, then slid a long long way before clattering to a standstill. It took the stranger less time to twist her arm behind her back and right up between her shoulder blades.

"I'd like to think you were touching me up for the sheer pleasure of it, but something tells me that's not it. How about you tell me what *is* going on?"

He stood close behind her, close enough that the words washed over her nape in a warm wave. She shook her head to rid herself of the sensation, and he stretched her arm further.

"Ouch," she breathed. "You're hurting me."

"You think that piece of plastic you were brandishing hasn't bruised me?" He released the pressure on her arm, although he didn't let it go. Long fingers manacled her wrist. "Well?" he prompted.

T.C. frowned. If he knew the gun was fake, it explained his casual attitude, but why hadn't he called her on it? And why had he asked *her* to explain? She wrenched her arm and found herself hauled backward, right up hard against his body, so when he spoke his voice hummed close against her ear. "All right, sweet hands, if you don't want to tell me why you're skulking about in the dark, I'll have to start searching for clues."

His hand slid over her hip. T.C. yelped and tried to swat it away, but he pulled her nearer by banding an arm around her chest. Her back was pasted to his front, so close that when he laughed, the low sound vibrated from his chest into her body. It set up a resonant buzz along her spine, like a tuning fork perfectly pitched.

Or maybe that was in reaction to the hand cruising down one thigh then back up again, inch by leisurely inch. Omigosh, now it was inside her pajama coat, sliding across her belly. She wriggled frantically, needing to escape his touch—but wriggling was a big mistake. It brought her backside up hard against his thighs. All the breath left her lungs in a rush.

"What's the matter, sweetheart? Not used to having a perfect stranger run his hands all over you? Intrusive, isn't it?"

"My name's not sweet *anything!*" She kicked out, and the sudden flurry of legs and boots caught him unaware. The arm holding her slipped, and she swiveled sideways; his free hand grabbed...and closed over her left breast.

For a long second they both went completely still. T.C. heard the rasp of her own breathing, not quite steady, over the heavy thud of her heartbeat. Then she kicked out again, and this time her booted heel caught him in the shin.

He swore succinctly, and T.C. felt a rush of vindictive satisfaction. This was his fault. He shouldn't have been touching her at all, let alone in that deliberate way. She swung her feet again, and he grunted as he shifted sideways to avoid her heels.

He cursed again. "What are you, half mule? Stop kicking, for Pete's sake!"

"Then...let...me...go!"

"I'll let you go when I can see what you're up to. Where's the light switch?"

When she didn't answer his arm tightened. "Down there...straight ahead...last door on your left." T.C.'s in-

structions came out in reluctant grunts against the arm
crushing her diaphragm.

He frog-marched her the length of the breezeway,
pushed open the door to her quarters and flicked the
switch. T.C. squeezed her eyes shut against the sudden
brightness. Dazzling yellow figures danced across the
backs of her lids. She heard Ug yap a greeting, the scratch
of her nails as she scampered across the concrete floor,
then felt the little dog bouncing around her legs...no, make
that *their* legs.

*Oh, great. First my dog doesn't even hear him arrive,
then she greets him like a long-lost friend!*

"Down. Sit." His instructions were so do-not-argue that
T.C. almost sat herself.

Needless to say, her traitorous dog subsided.

The stranger's grip eased. His hands moved to her
shoulders, swinging her around until she stood staring into
his broad chest. Her nose almost touched the front of his
shirt and the chest hair revealed by two open buttons.

She swallowed with difficulty and raised a hand to push
against the solid wall of his chest. It didn't budge. Beneath
her palm beat the steady pulse of his heart. She tipped her
head back, found herself too close to see anything beyond a chin dark with regrowth and centered with a faint
familiar-looking cleft.

Oh, no, it couldn't be....

She backed up until the full lips and long, straight nose
came into focus; then she closed her eyes.

Oh, yes, it most definitely was!

"Tell me I didn't just kick Nick Corelli in the shins,"
she said on the end of a long tortured groan. *Tell me I
didn't just run my hands all over Nick Corelli's body.* Except she knew she had—the knowledge still tingled in the
palms of those hands.

She opened her eyes to find his focused intently on her,
and for a long moment she could do nothing but stare back.

His eyes weren't obsidian dark like all the Corellis she had met but the pure cerulean of a summer sky. So unexpected, so unusual, so giddily, perfectly beautiful. Finally she remembered to take another breath, to close the mouth she feared had fallen open in gobstopped awe.

"You know me?" He sounded startled by that, and there was definitely surprise lurking in those amazing eyes. Surprise and something more. Interest? Or merely curiosity?

She shook her head, as much to clear her stunned senses as in reply. "We've never met, but I recognize you. From photographs. Your father showed me photographs."

"You recognized me instantly from a couple of pictures?"

More than a couple. T.C. felt herself color as she recalled how many...and how often she'd pored over them. Good grief, she had actually freeze-framed a video of his sister's wedding on one spectacular shot. It was a wonder she hadn't pegged him as Nick the Gorgeous One in the total dark!

"I take it you aren't a burglar. Do you work here?" He glanced down at where Ug lay at his feet—almost *on* his feet—and grinned. "Let me guess. You're security, and this is your guard dog."

T.C.'s heart did a slow motion flip-flop as the effect of that lazy drawl, the warmth of that slow grin, rippled through her body. She couldn't help her automatic response. How could she *not* smile back at him? How could she watch one quizzically arched brow disappear behind the thick fall of his hair and *not* think about combing it back from his face?

Belatedly she realized that the brow had arched in question. Asking what? Something about her working here? "Um...I'm the trainer. I train Joe's horses."

His expression changed from quizzical to startled in one blink of his dark lashes. "*You're* Tamara Cole?"

"That's me."

He inspected her with unnerving thoroughness, starting at her boots and working all the way up her legs and body. When he arrived back at her face, he let out a choked sort of snort that sounded like equal parts disbelief and suppressed laughter, and the warmth suffusing T.C.'s veins turned prickly with irritation. She knew she wasn't looking her best, but that was no reason for him to shake his head and grin as if he couldn't quite believe what his eyes were telling him. She folded her arms and regarded him as coolly as the hot flush of mortification allowed. "What are you doing here, Nick?"

"Apart from being attacked by a crazy little horse-training woman dressed in pajamas and boots?"

"I mean," she said tightly, as he continued to grin down at her, "I've been waiting to hear from someone for weeks and weeks, but I didn't expect *you*. Last I heard, you were lost in the wilds of Alaska."

The grin faded. "Who told you that?"

"George mentioned it. After the funeral." She shrugged off the memory of that short, unpleasant meeting. *Who-told-who-what* didn't matter when important questions remained unanswered. Like, what was Nick doing here, and why had he arrived unannounced in the middle of the night? "You should have let me know you were coming."

"I've been trying to do that for the last six hours." With disturbing accuracy he homed in on her telephone and picked up the receiver she'd left off the hook. "I don't suppose this has anything to do with the constant busy signal?"

"I must have bumped it. Or something."

He stared at her for a full ten seconds, then gestured with the instrument in his hand. "Is this on the same line as the house?"

T.C. cleared her throat, told herself it was ridiculous to feel such a sharp frisson of apprehension at the sight of a

phone, at the thought of it being able to ring and ring and
ring.... "Yes. There's only the one line."

"Then if it's all the same to you, I'd prefer we keep
that line open." As he cradled the receiver, the meaning
behind his words gelled. If he needed a phone, he must be
staying.

"Why are you here, Nick?" she blurted. "I expected
George, or that solicitor with the bullfrog eyes."

The corners of Nick's mouth twitched. "We used to call
him Kermit."

T.C. tried to ignore the mental image of Kermit in pin-
stripes but failed. And as they smiled in shared amusement,
as she had done so many times with his father, T.C. knew
why Nick was here. It made perfect sense that Joe would
leave the place of his heart to the son of his heart, the one
he had spoken of with such obvious love.

It also explained the delay. Nick—self-indulgent, free-
wheeling Nick—had disappeared on some wilderness skiing jaunt the day his father was hospitalized. Joe lingered
ten more days, but Nick didn't come home.

As she collected Ug from the floor and hugged the dog's
furry warmth close against her chest, T.C. felt the tight
twist of pain for the man who had been her boss, her men-
tor and her savior—and the strong sting of resentment for
the son who had let him down.

Nick watched as a sheen of moisture quelled the sea-
green intensity of her gaze, and he felt a sharp kick of
response, a need to ease the pain he glimpsed in those
spectacular eyes. He actually took a step forward, but she
nailed him to the spot with a fierce look that reminded him
of his bruised ribs and scraped shin. He gave himself a
mental tap on the head.

What was he thinking?

Jet lag must be kicking in if he thought she needed
comforting. The pale cap of baby-soft hair, the cute little
nose, the huge eyes—they were all a deception. This little

firebrand had a tough streak a mile wide. His gaze slid to her lips for at least the tenth time since he'd flicked the light switch. Full and soft, with a distinct inclination to pout, there was absolutely nothing tough about them. They looked downright kissable...until they tightened savagely. Nick cleared his mind of all kissing-thoughts as he cleared his throat. "So, Tamara..."

"What did you call me?"

"Tamara. That *is* your name, isn't it? Or would you rather I kept on calling you *sweet hands?*"

"You can call me T.C."

"That's hardly a name, just a couple of initials. I think I'll stick with Tamara."

Her lush lips compressed into an angry bow, and Nick felt a sudden spike of stimulation. It was the kind of buzz he'd chased across continents, from challenge to challenge and from woman to woman. The kind he hadn't felt for too many years, and he didn't understand where the feeling was coming from.

Apart from her mouth and the way those big eyes sparked green fire, Tamara Cole didn't come close to his type. He liked women who slid out of bed with silk clinging to their curves. He liked women who knew they were women. Must be jet lag—that was the only explanation. That and the fact that George had got her all wrong. From his description, Nick had imagined big hair, a big blowzy body, an even bigger attitude. She surely had the attitude, but her blond hair was cropped boyishly short, and, frankly, there wasn't a whole lot of body.

Just a nice little handful.

He allowed that sensory memory to drum through his blood for a whole minute before he reminded himself how deceptive appearances could be. George was a prime example. Just because Tamara Cole didn't fit George's description of the shrewd opportunist who had wriggled her way into Joe's life as well as his bed—just because the very thought had caused his earlier guffaw of amusement—didn't mean she hadn't done just that.

"Why are you here, Nick?"

Her question cut into Nick's reverie, and he pretended to consider it as he strolled over to her bed, tested the mattress, sat and swung his legs up. He picked up her pillow and propped it between his head and the wall.

"Why am I here?" He regarded her bottom lip through half-closed eyes, and the low-grade buzz in his veins intensified. "I'm here to meet you...*partner.*"

Two

"**P**art-ner?" T.C.'s voice cracked midword, so the second syllable came out squeaky. She tried to control her trembling legs but failed miserably, and the nearest storage trunk came up to meet her backside with an audible thump, jolting Ug from her arms. "What do you mean by *partner?*" Her voice sounded as weak as her knees felt.

"Standard definition. Two persons, sharing equally."

Oh, no. Joe, you didn't. You couldn't. You wouldn't.
"Sharing what…exactly?"

"This place."

T.C. swallowed, ran her tongue around her dry mouth. "You're saying Joe left me half of Yarra Park?"

"And everything on it, four-legged and otherwise. You have a problem with that?"

"Of course I do. It's too much, too…" Her throat constricted around the words, and she had to stop, to swallow twice before she could continue. "I don't understand. Why didn't he say something? Why hasn't *anyone* said anything?''

''There was a clause in the will…. Joe requested that I come here and tell you.''

That made about as much sense as the rest of it.

T.C. shook her head slowly. *Oh, Joe, why did you do this?* She jerked to her feet and must have walked to the window, because she found herself staring into the aluminum-framed square of night. She forced herself to look beyond her stunned senses, beyond the thick emotion that constricted her chest and blurred her vision.

Why?

Her boss had been a steady, almost ponderous, thinker— this couldn't be some whim. He had also been devoted to his large family to such an extent that he had often lamented spoiling them with a too-easy lifestyle. Staring into the dark, she recalled their hostility the day of Joe's funeral, and for the first time she understood where it had come from. She had been in that same place. She knew how it felt to be overlooked in favor of a virtual stranger.

''I imagine your family has a problem with it,'' she said slowly.

''You could say they're less than thrilled with our little windfall.''

T.C. whirled around. ''Don't call it that! I didn't expect anything. I don't *want* anything.'' She spread her arms wide in an imploring gesture. ''Why did he do this, Nick?''

''Gee, I don't know, Tamara. Some might assume it's because you were *very* good at your job.''

Heat flooded T.C.'s cheeks, then ebbed just as rapidly. Surely he couldn't mean what that suggestive drawl implied…could he? Stunned, she stared at him, taking in his laid-back posture, the mocking half grin, and the heat returned in a flash of red.

''*Yesss!*'' The word came out a long, low hiss as she

advanced on him. "I *am* very good at my job—that's why Joe employed me—so I hope you're not insinuating I earned this *windfall* doing anything besides training horses." She reached down and wrenched the pillow from behind him, then seriously contemplated koshing him over the head with it.

"Hey, take it easy. I said *some* might assume."

The *some* most likely encompassed the rest of Joe's family but apparently didn't include Nick—that was why he had been so taken aback when he learned her identity. What had he called her? *A crazy little horse-training woman in pajamas and boots.* The thought of anyone wanting to bed *that* must really have tickled him.

Not having to prove the nature of her relationship with Joe should have delighted T.C., so why did she feel so…slighted? Annoyed with her contrary feelings, she tossed the pillow aside. It didn't matter what Nick Corelli thought of her; it mattered that he was lounging on her bed, treating Joe's bequest with a complete lack of respect.

"What about your part in this, Nick? What did your family make of that?"

"They shared the rest of Joe's fortune." He shrugged negligently. "I guess I got the consolation prize."

Hands on hips, she took a step forward and looked down on him with all the scorn that comment deserved. "You feel you deserved a prize?"

He tipped his head back against the bare concrete wall, eyes narrowed, expression no longer amused. "Meaning?"

"Meaning where were you when your father needed you? When your brother and sisters took turns sitting by his hospital bed for days on end? It was *you* he wanted there, Nick. *You* he asked for. And where were you? Oh, that's right, you had some dinky mountain to ski!"

Slowly he unfolded his long frame and rose to his feet. His eyes glittered darkly, a muscle ticked at the corner of his mouth, and without conscious thought T.C. took a step back. But when he spoke his voice was cool and flat. "George told you that?"

She swallowed, nodded, wondered what nerve she had struck.

"Did he tell you how much effort he put into finding me? That he didn't even bother leaving a message with my service?"

"He shouldn't have had to find you."

"I should have known Joe was sick...how?"

T.C. flushed. Joe hadn't told a soul about his diagnosis. No one had guessed until it was too late.

"I'm sorry, Nick." And because the words sounded totally inadequate, or maybe because the dark emotion in his eyes—the hurt, anger, regret—echoed somewhere deep within, she reached out and placed her hand on his arm.

"Yeah, well, it's history now." Nick shrugged off both her apology and the touch of her fingers. He didn't need her awkward attempt at sympathy any more than he needed his own sense of frustration at what might have been. Both were pointless. Abruptly he swung around, away from the mix of compassion and confusion that gleamed in her eyes. He needed something else to focus his frustration on, and he found it right before his eyes in the stark concrete walls, the uncarpeted floor and make-do furniture, the clothes discarded atop packing trunks.

"Why are you living here?"

She shook her head slightly. "What do you mean?"

"George said you used to live in the house but you'd moved out, I assumed to somewhere off the farm. Why the hell would you move out of the house into this rathole?"

"I didn't feel right staying in the house," she said stiffly.

"Couldn't you find anywhere better than this?"

"I didn't have any—" She stopped abruptly, changing tack with a forced casualness that didn't fool Nick for a second. "I needed to be here, near the horses. It's no big deal."

"George should have told me you were living here."

Except how could he, when Nick hadn't given him a chance? When he'd grown so frustrated by the man's smoothly evasive replies that he threw his hands in the air and walked out, jumped in his car and drove straight here?

He scrubbed a hand over his face and wondered what had happened to his logic, which seemed to have gone missing...probably to the same place as his usual even temper. He adopted a more reasonable tone before he continued. "If I'd known you were living here, I wouldn't have been surprised to see your light."

"So that's why you came down here." Her smile was edged with relief, as if she'd needed an explanation...or because the conversation had taken a safer turn. "Something woke me, but I wasn't sure what, so I turned the light out again. When I heard you outside, it scared about a year off my life."

"Sorry about that. I guess we both had the wrong handle on each other."

Whatever the reason for her smile, it sliced a swathe through Nick's irritability, made it possible for him to smile right back at her. And he found something in her expression, in the slow color that highlighted her cheekbones, that reminded him what sort of a handle they'd had on each other in the close darkness of the breezeway. Her hands sliding over his shirt, touching his jeans. His hand on her belly, her breast. Heat licked through him like wildfire, doing more than sear his blood vessels. It surprised the hell out of him.

Jet lag, he reminded himself as he shoved his hands in his jacket pockets and cleared his throat. "You want to pack a few things—what you need for tonight?"

She stiffened visibly. "I beg your pardon?"

"You're not staying here."

"I'm perfectly comfortable here."

Her mutt, which had fallen asleep on the foot of her bed, chose that moment to whimper and twitch. Nick snorted. "Your *dog* isn't even comfortable here."

"Must we discuss this now?"

"No. We can discuss it later...*after* we've moved you."

When he started toward her, she held up a hand. "Look, it's the middle of the night. I don't want to fight with you, and I don't want to have to make up another bed. Okay?"

Nick dragged a hand through his hair. Unfortunately he could see her point. "Fine," he conceded. "But tomorrow you're moving out of here."

"Shouldn't sorting out this ridiculous bequest be our first priority?"

Nick frowned at her choice of adjective. *Unexpected*, yes. *Unusual*, maybe. *Overly generous*, definitely. "You think it's ridiculous?"

"It makes no sense."

"You can't think of any reason why Joe would leave you a million-dollar bequest?"

All the color leached from her face as she stared back at him. In his world, a million dollars didn't turn a hair; to Tamara Cole, the figure was obviously staggering. Buying her out would be as simple as writing a check, Nick realized. So where was the satisfaction that always accompanied knowledge of a sure thing, a deal all but closed? As she continued to stare at him, wide-eyed and unblinking, he noticed she looked more than stunned. She looked as dead beat as he felt.

"Sleep on it, green eyes," he advised as he headed to the door. "We'll talk later."

"Nick."

He stilled, one hand on the doorknob. Now why should the sound of his name on her tongue cause his pulse to pound? All his responses seemed shot to bits tonight.

"I'm sorry about before, about mistaking you for a burglar."

Nick turned, caught her looking at him with that same expression as before, the one that made him think about hands in the dark and the sweet little body hidden beneath unflattering flannel. He stared back, a slow grin on his lips and a fast burn in his gut.

"I'm not."

After the door clicked shut, T.C. rested her overheated face against the cool windowpane and one hand against her overstimulated heart. No man's smile should be allowed to have such an effect, and especially not a man so out of her league.

It wasn't fair, but it wasn't unexpected.

From his photos, she knew the man was gorgeous, from Joe's stories she'd learned of his charm, but nothing could have prepared her for Nick Corelli in the flesh. Nothing could have prepared her for that blue gaze sliding over her like a silk blanket, warming her, sensitizing every cell in her skin, as he murmured "I'm not." As if he had enjoyed their tussle in the dark, as if the surge of attraction she had felt so intensely was mutual. As if a man who could take his pick of the glamorous, the beautiful and the smart, would be interested in her.

As if!

With a snort of derision, she turned her face against the windowpane and looked outside in time to see the house windows light up one by one, marking his progress through the entry hall into the living area, and then on to the bedrooms. A tug of alarm pulled her hard up against the glass. Which would he choose?

"Please. Not my room, not my bed," she breathed. "It's enough knowing you're in my home."

Whoa! When, precisely, had she started calling Joe's house her home? Sure, she had lived in it the past five

years, but only because Joe insisted, only because he was
the kind of man who brooked no argument.

"You think a house like this deserves to be empty? You
think I want to come here to an empty house after a whole
week spent with too many *idioti* for any one man's patience?"

The backs of her eyes pricked at the memory of Joe's
words, and she pressed her lids tightly closed. She hadn't
cried once in those god-awful months since she'd finally
learned of her boss's terminal illness, and she wasn't going
to start shedding tears now.

*If you don't want to be treated like a girl, don't cry like
one.* That came straight from her father's concise book of
lessons, right after *There's only one thing a man like that
could want from a girl like you.*

She had been young and reckless when she learned the
harsh truth of her father's words. She had given that one
thing to a rich, smooth-talking, heartbreaker named Miles
Newman, and after he laughed at her words of love and
moved on to the new stable girl, she'd dried the last of
her girl-tears and thrown away the handkerchief.

Never again would she trade her self-respect for something she mistook for love. Never again would she mistake
the flashfire of physical attraction for something more. Oh,
she wanted there to be somebody—a special person to
share her life, to love and to cherish—but she didn't need
the palpitations and the heartache and the tears. She needed
strength and stability. She needed respect and understanding and companionship. Until she found a man with those
qualities, she would make do with her own company.

Except at this moment her own company was making
her edgy and unsettled. She swung away from the window
and started to pace her room, but that activity did nothing
to ease her restlessness. The quarters she had accepted as
adequate now felt cold, dank and claustrophobic. The clut-
ter she stepped over and around every day now looked like

a sad chaotic mess. She jammed her eyes shut and cursed Nick Corelli for this new perspective, then cursed herself double-time for caring. His opinion of her living conditions shouldn't matter one blue-eyed damn. But when she opened her eyes they were focused on her bed, and she could still see his long denim-encased legs spread across it. She could still imagine his body heat seeping into the covers.

With a growl of frustration she strode to the door and hauled it open. A horse whickered softly across the way, instantly easing the tightness in her chest. She pulled the door to behind her and moved surefootedly toward the lone equine head that loomed over its stable door.

"Hey, Star." She smiled as she rubbed the proffered jaw, then let her fingers dwell on the velvet warmth of the animal's muzzle. Warm, familiar, soothing. She felt her tense muscles relax another degree, felt her smile kick up a notch. "Don't you ever sleep?" she crooned as she ran her other hand along the mare's neck and under her blanket, automatically checking for warmth.

The mare stalked off with an impatient shake of her head, then circled the box with her long graceful strides. She, Tamara Cole, owned half of this fabulous animal. Shivering with a flash of intense excitement as much as the cold, T.C. shoved her hands deep into her pockets. "No," she told herself firmly. "You know you can't accept it."

And if she didn't accept it, what would happen? She wondered if Joe had considered that possibility and if he had made some provision, named some alternate benefactor. Nick hadn't mentioned it, but then, he hadn't mentioned much at all, and she had been too stunned to think coherently.

Now a whole crowd of questions scrambled for answers. Why had George told her to carry on as usual, knowing she was now a part-owner? Why had Joe made her a part-owner, knowing she would likely refuse the gift? Why had he specifically requested she learn the news from Nick?

Frowning, she turned to lean her back against the stable door. It didn't surprise her that Joe hadn't left Yarra Park to any of his Melbourne-based family. Neither George nor any of his sisters had ever shown any interest in the property—in fact, they had bemoaned their father's obsession with horses. An old man's eccentricity, George had called it, with a condescending twist of his lips.

Nor did it surprise her that he had singled out Nick, the only one who had chosen his own career path in preference to a ready-made position in a Corelli company. At first that decision had caused a rift, but ultimately Nick's independent success had earned his father's respect and admiration. It made sense that Joe would consider Nick worthy of his beloved property, but would Nick appreciate the magnitude of the gift?

T.C. snorted. He called it a consolation prize, for heaven's sake.

Frankly she couldn't see what he would want with a fledgling standardbred training establishment at the opposite end of the world from his New York base, and if he didn't want his half, what should she do about hers?

She blew out a breath and shook her head slowly. "Gee, Joe, it'd be really good if you could help me out here…if you could tell me what you were thinking when you drafted that will." Of course, no magical answer boomed out from beyond the steel rafters. "Seems like I'll have to do this the hard way," she told Star, knowing exactly how difficult that would be.

First she would have to deal with her treacherous body's intense physical response to Nick's presence, and then her awestruck mind might kick into gear and form some meaningful connection with her mouth. Maybe then she would be capable of asking all the questions that needed answering before she could decide what to do.

Three

T.C. intended posing those questions the next time she saw Nick. She planned to stiffen her backbone, look him in the eye and say, "Nick, I need to know your intentions."

She was pleased with that forthright opener, composed the next morning while she and Jason, her stable hand, exercised the first half of their team. And when it was time for a coffee break, she took her mug to an upturned bucket in the breezeway, tilted her face toward the midmorning sun and fine-tuned her intonation.

"Nick, I *need* to know...Nick, I need *to know*..."

Then Nick sauntered into the barn, and her plans, her intonation and her backbone, turned to mush. He wore a polo shirt in the same azure-blue as his eyes, and faded jeans that hugged him in all the right places. The warmth that flooded her body had nothing to do with the sun. Her heart stalled, then bounded into overdrive. She felt all the same jittery reactions as when she stepped a horse onto the track before a big race, but she didn't look away. She couldn't *not* watch his lazy loose-limbed approach. Talk about poetry in slow motion. If he'd been a horse, she would have labeled him a fabulous mover.

"Is this the new boss?" Jason asked.

T.C. nodded, swallowed, inhaled once, exhaled once. By then Nick was close enough for her to notice his shower-damp hair and the rested look about his eyes. It was obvious *his* sleep hadn't been disturbed by spicy aftertones clinging to his pillow!

Somehow she managed to mumble the necessary introductions, and Nick shook Jason's hand. "You must own the one-two-five out front."

Very smooth opening, T.C. thought with a cynical twist of her mouth, seeing as Jason was mad-keen on his newly acquired dirt bike. They swapped notes in that rev-head shorthand T.C. had never understood, and when Ug snuffled noisily out of her morning nap, Nick hunkered down to tickle her behind the ears. With a fatuous look of bliss clouding her mismatched eyes, the dog promptly rolled onto her back.

T.C. snorted. She bet females did that trick for Nick Corelli all the time.

"What do you call her?" His gaze lifted from the prone dog and met T.C.'s over the rim of her coffee mug.

"Ug." Jason supplied the answer, which was just as well, because the smiling warmth in Nick's eyes had struck T.C. dumb. Behind the subterfuge of sipping coffee, she attempted to unravel the knot in her tongue.

"Strange name." He smiled right into her eyes, and that uncooperative tongue looped itself in a second half-hitch. Luckily Jason came to her rescue again.

"When Joe first brought her home—he found her down the road a bit—T.C. said she wanted to call her Lucky, because she was lucky Joe found her. But Joe says 'There's nothin' lucky about a dog that looks like that.'"

"So how did she get to be Ug?" Nick asked.

"Joe said 'I'd call her plain old ugly,' and it just sort of stuck. Except T.C. shortened it to Ug."

T.C. smiled at the familiar anecdote. She felt like she might finally be capable of speech. "You look like you slept well," she said, by way of a start.

"Like a baby." His smile deepened the creases on either side of his mouth, and it struck her that he must smile a lot. "Any more of that coffee around?"

"I'll get it," Jason offered. "Um, you want milk or anythin'?"

"The works." Somehow T.C. wasn't surprised. She figured Nick would demand *the works* in all kinds of ways. "Plenty of milk, at least two sugars. Thanks, Jason."

As the kid bustled off, Nick hoped the coffee wasn't already bubbling away in a percolator. He wanted some time alone with Tamara. He pulled up the bucket vacated by Jason and sat. "You know, I'd still be sleeping like a baby except the phone rang."

She stopped fidgeting with her mug and went very still. "I didn't hear it. I guess we were down at the track. Was the call for me?"

"I can't say. There was no one there."

She cradled the mug in both hands as if to steady it, declared, "Probably a wrong number," then swiveled around to peer down the alleyway. "I wonder what's keeping Jason?"

Nick gritted his teeth. Her evasiveness was already roughing the edges of his patience. "If it was a boyfriend calling," he suggested slowly, "I might have put him off."

"If I had a boyfriend, he'd know not to call when it's short odds I'd be down at the track."

When he met her hostile glare, Nick felt a perverse satisfaction, and it had nothing to do with the no-boyfriend revelation. Finally he had her attention. "Seems to me there's something funny going on with your telephone. No one there this morning, off the hook yesterday.''

"Geez, T.C.'' Neither had heard Jason's approach. He stood there, shaking his head reproachfully. "Did you leave it off the hook again?'' He handed Nick his coffee. "She did that the other day, too.''

The warning glare she directed at Jason told Nick his instincts were spot on. "Perhaps you had better explain.''

"Explain what? I knocked the receiver off the hook and didn't notice. You got a wrong number. End of story.'' With a dismissive shrug, she turned to Jason. "You can show Nick around while I finish the jogging.''

Nick stopped her intended exit with a hand on her shoulder. "Have you been getting nuisance calls?''

When she shuffled from foot to foot without answering, Nick increased the pressure on her shoulder. Over the top of her head he met Jason's worried look and smiled reassuringly. "How about you carry on with the horses while I sort this out?''

As Jason set off, whistling cheerfully, he felt her tense up beneath his hand. "You've been here less than twelve hours and you're giving directions to my staff?''

"Our staff,'' he corrected.

She let out her breath in a soft whoosh. "We have to talk about that.''

"Yes, we do. But first we're going to settle the phone business.''

She bit her bottom lip, and Nick waited a count of ten while she considered. "So, okay, there has been the odd anonymous call.''

"How long has this been going on?''

She shrugged. "A couple of weeks. On and off.''

"A couple of *weeks!* Have you reported it?''

"Look, there's nothing to report. No threats, no heavy breathing. Probably just kids mucking about. It's no big deal.''

"No?" Nick swore beneath his breath, then out loud when the penny dropped. "That's why you attacked me last night. You thought I was the caller. What if you'd been right? What if I *had* been some stalker hell-bent on hurting you? Did you think of that before you confronted me with that damn fool toy?"

"I can look after myself. I've been looking after my-self—"

"Is that what you think you were doing when you ran your hands all over me last night?" He grabbed her hand and pulled it to him, forcing her to touch him, then to stroke down his chest from collarbone to waist in one long, slow sensuous caress. "When you touched me like this?"

She recoiled as if she had contacted a live wire, then stood blinking her huge green eyes at him. She rubbed the hand he had used to demonstrate his point down her thigh as if trying to remove his imprint from her skin.

That notion was as powerfully erotic as her actual touch.

With a proud lift of her chin, she drew herself up as tall as her diminished height allowed and met his gaze. "I did not touch you like that," she said with quiet dignity.

"You might as well have," Nick muttered, and gri-maced at the uncomfortable tightness of his jeans as she turned on her heel and walked away, her backbone rigid, head held high. He watched her until she disappeared out the front of the barn, and then he shook his head in disgust.

Well, hell, didn't that little demonstration come off a treat?

All he had managed to prove was how easily she could fire up his temper and heat his blood. He had come out here this morning to get the phone business sorted, to smooth over their rocky start with some getting-to-know-you dialogue, then to move her back into the house. After lunch he wanted to check the balance sheet valuations to ensure the offer he made to buy her out was fair. And after dinner, once business was out of the way, his getting-to-know-you plans were aimed purely at pleasure.

So far he had barely managed to tackle item one on his list—not exactly a grade-A start. Then he relived the touch of her hand, recalled the hot spark in her eyes and the soft color in her cheeks, and he smiled. He had some work in front of him to get to that last pleasurable item, but it would be worth the effort.

Yep, it would take both work and flexibility, and when Jason came by leading a horse, Nick saw an opportunity to adapt his plans. Chances were he would learn more from the kid in an hour than he could finesse from Tamara in a day.

"Need some help?" he asked as Jason tethered the animal to a hitching rail.

"You know how to bandage?"

Nick counted four rolls in Jason's hands and smiled easily. "I'm a quick study. You show me the first one, and I figure I can manage the rest."

T.C. eased Monte's leg down, stretched out the kink in her back and tried to prevent her gaze straying to the other end of the barn. What were they laughing about *this* time? They'd been at it for more than an hour, chatting easily, laughing with nerve-grating regularity, Jason obviously reveling in his role as teacher to Nick's student. Their rapport shouldn't rankle. Nick could spread his charm from here to the back of beyond, but as long as he didn't try it on her, what should she care?

With a last disgruntled glance in their direction, she stooped down, took Monte's leg again and eased it between her knees, determined to refocus on rasping a level surface for the horseshoe. She managed to concentrate for all of three minutes before she heard the slow tread of approaching boots, then the scrape of a drum against concrete. Looking back beneath her arm, she saw the out-stretched length of denim-clad legs as he took a seat.

Ignore him, she warned her body, but to no avail. Already her muscles had tightened in unconscious response to his proximity, to the notion of him watching her. So okay, she told herself, the man unnerves you, but he's right there, not six feet away, and it's about time you started on that list of questions. But as she shifted the words about in her mind, forcing them into some sort of logical order, her tension must have transmitted itself to Monte and he shifted his weight, almost overbalancing her.

By the time she righted herself and calmed Monte, she had decided this was neither the time nor the place for this conversation. Much too important for casual asides between hammer blows, she justified, attacking Monte's hoof with renewed fervor because she wanted the job finished—quickly. She could practically feel the touch of that warm blue gaze on her backside every time she bent into her task, but she clenched her jaw firmly, determined not to show how much he disconcerted her.

"What are you doing?" Nick asked after she had steadfastly ignored him for several minutes.

"Rasping."

"I can see that much."

"Glad your eyesight's not a problem," she mumbled.

"Nothing wrong with my eyesight...fortunately."

She let the horse's leg down and tsked with disgust as she strode to the anvil seated on a nearby workbench and started bashing at the horseshoe. "Haven't you anything better to do than ogle my backside?" *Bash. Bash. Bash.*

"You think I was ogling?"

She stopped hammering long enough to cast him a long-suffering look.

"I hardly ever ogle a woman with a hammer in her hand. Too dangerous."

She almost smiled at that. Almost. Nick wondered why

she fought the urge, wondered what it would take to hear her laugh out loud. He had a feeling he would enjoy seeing her emotive eyes brimming with laughter even more than he enjoyed them sparking with irritation.

"I hope it doesn't bother you, me sitting here, watching you."

"Actually it does." Tossing the hammer aside, she turned around to face him. "I'm not used to having anyone watch me work."

"Joe didn't?"

"He...he didn't make me feel uncomfortable." And Nick did. He could see the uneasiness in her gaze, in the restless way she shifted her weight from one hip to the other, in the way she scuffed the toe of one boot against the ground.

"You must have gotten along pretty well with Joe," he said before she could turn away again. He didn't mind if her discomfort was due to her awareness of him, but he did want her comfortable enough to talk with him. Joe seemed like the place to start.

"Because he left me so much?"

"That's not what I meant."

One corner of her mouth curled cynically. "No?"

"No. You say you weren't lovers, but obviously you were closer than the usual boss-employee."

Their eyes met and held, and he saw a flicker of something—maybe surprise, maybe relief, maybe some kind of yielding—before she looked away. He saw her swallow, then take a deep breath, before she spoke in a slow, measured voice.

"Joe gave me this job at a time when I really needed it, and he did so against everyone's advice. I knew horses, but I'd never managed a stable this size. I was young and inexperienced, plus I was female. But he went with his gut instinct, and he gave me the job." A ghost of a smile curved her lips and touched Nick somewhere deep inside, somewhere he didn't even want to identify. "I made sure he never regretted that decision, and he appreciated the extra effort I put in. We weren't lovers, but we built a bond."

"Of mutual respect?"

She looked up then, and the intensity in her eyes smacked him hard, midchest. "I don't know about the mutual, but I do know how much I respected Joe. I admired him, I loved him, I wished he was my father." The last phrase came out in a breathy rush. Then, as if she regretted letting on so much, she turned her head and looked away.

"You said Joe gave you a job at a time when you really needed it. You were broke?"

"In more ways than you can imagine."

Silently Nick willed her to go on, to tell him something of the past that shadowed her voice.

"I won't bore you with the long story. Suffice it to say my esteem had taken a pounding and this job was exactly what I needed. I'm not talking about finding employment or the money—it was the responsibility and the trust. It was his belief in me."

She turned abruptly and stomped back to the horse, leaving Nick standing there weighed down by the intensity of her words and his own memories. He had experienced that same aching need. Hell, he'd spent the first eight years of his life with no one caring for him, let alone believing in him, so it had taken him a long time to recognize those gifts as the most precious Joe had given him when he took him into his family and called him his second son.

"Yeah," he muttered hoarsely to himself. "I wish he'd been my father, too."

He found her back at work, nailing the shoe with businesslike efficiency, as if she had already shed the emotion that still knotted Nick's gut. That irritated him almost as much as how she had walked away. He watched her swat a fly from the horse's belly, and with half an eye noticed the animal had worked its lead undone. It didn't seem to be going anywhere—in fact, it looked like it had fallen asleep. What was it with her animals and sleep?

"Why don't you get a farrier to do that?" he asked.

"Pay someone to do something I can do? I don't think so."

"Why do something so tough and painstaking when you can pay someone to do it?" he countered.

She looked up, her eyes sharp with disdain. "That's not my way of doing things."

Trying to prove her toughness, Nick guessed. Not because she was young and inexperienced, but because she was female. There was a story here, a history he suddenly needed to know. "What *is* your way, Tamara?"

No answer. Okay. He would try a different tack.

"How did you learn to farrier?"

"My father taught me."

"Your father's a horseman?"

"He was."

That was it. No further explanation, and, dammit, her reticence intrigued him as much as it irritated him. "So you followed the family tradition into horse training?"

In one smooth movement she turned, drew the horse's leg forward and rested the hoof on her thigh. "I chose this profession because I love it. Tradition had nothing to do with it."

Nick inspected her closely drawn brows, the flare of her nostrils, her tense grip on the hammer. "For someone who loves her job, you don't look like you're having much fun."

Eyes almost crossed with consternation, she glared up at him, but before she could respond the horse swung its head and nipped her neatly on the backside. She yelped and leaped sideways, and when Nick grabbed her shoulders to pull her aside and then to steady her, he noticed the tears flooding her eyes. He also noticed that she wasn't rubbing her behind but was sucking her thumb.

"Hey, what's the matter?"

She slid the thumb from her mouth, and Nick felt the most unexpected rush of heat. Unexpected and unwarranted, given the circumstances. It was those lips, that damn pout.

"Here, let me see." Gently he took her hand and inspected the blood oozing from the base of her thumb. The sharp end of an unclinched nail had obviously dug in. "Do you have first-aid supplies?"

"It's only a scratch."

He silenced her with a look. "Sit down and don't move."

His authority didn't come from a raised voice but a certain don't-argue timbre. It had worked on Ug the previous night, and it worked on T.C. now. She sat on the drum. She didn't move. And when she looked up to find him standing, feet spread, hands on hips, glaring down at her, she told him where to find the first-aid kit.

"It's in the lunchroom—in the cupboard next to the fridge." She indicated the general direction with her good hand. He nodded grimly, pivoted, then stopped short when confronted by the ugly end of Monte. T.C. watched in amazement as he smacked the gelding's rump to turn him around, gathered up the lead and retethered it to the hitching rail before striding off.

Like he did it every day.

She didn't want to admire the man's competence—she had spent the last half hour deliberately not admiring anything about him—so she turned her attention to her thumb. Gingerly she wiggled it back and forth, reminding herself that the pain was all *his* fault.

If he hadn't disturbed her sleep, she wouldn't be so fuzzy-headed. If he hadn't forced her to touch him, her senses wouldn't be chock-full of memories of his hands on her. If he hadn't distracted her with his questions, she would have noticed Monte was loose.

So let him play Mr. Competence if he wanted. Maybe then he would go off and do something else—like leave her in peace.

Unfortunately his idea of playing Mr. Competence involved hunkering down in front of her and steadying himself with a hand on each of her knees. She could feel every degree of his body heat radiating through his long fingers, through her jeans and her skin, all the way into her flesh. For a man who moved with such lithe grace, he seemed to take an inordinate length of time to regain his balance and remove his hands.

Not that T.C. gained much respite. She had scarcely recovered her equilibrium before he picked up her hand, placed it palm-up in one of his and bent over to inspect her injury.

She stared at her hand lying in his. How small and soft it looked compared with his—exactly as he had described it in the early hours of the morning. She disliked that thought as much as she disliked the hitch in her breath as his thumb stroked across the center of her palm, tracing her lifeline. Or was that her heart line?

She closed her eyes and dragged in a breath, but instead of badly needed oxygen, her lungs filled with his soft musky scent. Dimly she thought about leaning forward and burying her nose in his neck...but then something akin to liquid fire hit her thumb, and she rose clean off the drum.

Nick steadied her with a hand on her elbow. "Sting a little?" he asked as he reapplied the antiseptic-soaked swab.

"Try a lot," she muttered shakily.

He leaned closer, so close that when he looked up, she could make out tiny flecks of gold in the blue of his irises. Then he smiled that brilliant world-tilting smile, and she couldn't help but return it.

"Good girl," he murmured, and for some dumb reason the admiration intermingled with concern in his eyes brought a thick lump to her throat. Tears welled in her eyes. To her chagrin, one spilled over and rolled down her cheek. She scrubbed at it with the back of her free hand, bit her lip, chanced a glance from beneath her lashes.

The hand on her elbow tightened for a second; then he bent over the first-aid kit at his feet. "We need to get this covered up."

He took longer than necessary to fix a plaster to her wound, as if he knew she needed time to collect herself and that she would find her tears humiliating. The thought of such insightfulness threatened her composure all over again. She shut her eyes and tried to concentrate on the pain—except there didn't seem to be much of that anymore.

"All right now?" His thumb gently stroked the inside of her wrist.

T.C. nodded, although she wasn't all right. For a start, there was that thumb stroking fire across her oversensitive skin. She knew his intent was solicitous rather than sensuous, but her senses weren't listening to reason. He moved, or she moved, or maybe the air around them moved, for she caught another heady whiff of his scent.

Burying her nose in his neck suddenly seemed like the only thing to do. With eyes still closed, she must have actually leaned in his direction, because the drum tipped forward and she would have toppled right into his lap but for a last second reflex that saw both her hands curl around his upper arms, her injury forgotten.

"Hey, no need to throw yourself at me."

His quip should have defused the awkwardness. T.C. did try to smile back, but her lips wouldn't cooperate. The sensation of taut muscles beneath her hands had turned her mouth desert-dry. She tried another smile, considered removing her hands, but couldn't manage either simple task.

And when she moistened her lips, his gaze followed the movement. His smile faded. There was a moment of intense gravity as they studied each other, and T.C. felt as if she was suspended in time and motion. As if her senses were too packed full of everything-Nick to allow anything else in.

Nearby a horse snorted, breaking the spell, and one corner of Nick's mouth kicked up. She could have escaped then, if she had wanted to. She didn't. She sat still, completely enmeshed in the slow-motion sequence. His hand reached toward her. His fingers combed a slow path through her hair, to her nape. He drew her face to his, gradually and surely, until their lips finally met.

His were warm, their touch soft and restrained, as if he were savoring that first contact as much as she. It was no more than lips meeting, touching, retreating, returning, yet it was the most exquisitely sensual indulgence of her life.

She whimpered low in her throat. His hand tightened on her neck, drew her mouth closer, while he slowly—oh so slowly—tasted his way around her lips, enticing them open, inviting her response, causing a cascade of delight to ripple through her body. He was leisurely, almost lazy, but he was very, very thorough. Around the edges of her hearing something jangled vaguely, but she shut it out, focusing all her senses on the complexities of a kiss she had never known existed.

Until he pulled away from her clinging lips.

Then she recognized the metallic strike of shod hooves on concrete, heard a low tuneless whistle, the clink of a steel bit. Jason returning from the track.

Four

Like a teenager caught necking, T.C. jumped to her feet, stumbling over her boots—or Nick's—in her clumsy haste.

"Jason's back," she said, only because she had to say something, to drop some words into the ever-deepening pool of silence.

"I did gather that."

"Yes, well, I should go help him."

"I'm sure he can manage," Nick said reasonably.

"Manage what?" Jason asked as he came into view. He pulled up short and frowned at T.C. "Thought you were going into town to watch Dave do that bone-chip op?"

Thank you, Jase! T.C. checked her watch and tossed an apologetic smile in Nick's general direction. "I lost all track of time. If I don't get moving, I'll be late."

"I need to pick up a few things in town. How about I drive and we can talk on the way?"

T.C. shook her head vehemently. "No. That's absolutely not necessary." She needed to get away from him, to cool the suffocating heat from her blood, to talk some common sense into her muddled mind. She had no right to be kissing Nick. Those kinds of luxuries belonged in fantasies, not in real life. ''I could be hours at the vet's, and then I have some shopping to do. I'm sure you have other plans for the afternoon.''

His lips set in a stubborn line, and she could imagine him picking her up and tossing her bodily into the passenger seat. A tempting frisson of anticipation scurried up her spine, and she retreated quickly, holding up a hand, as if that might keep it at bay.

''Look, I'm happy to shop for you. I know there's nothing in the house unless you brought supplies with you, and I can hardly imagine you packing bread and milk and tea bags.'' She was prattling about as quickly as she was backpedaling. She took a deep breath and made herself stop. ''I'm going to shower and change. Just write a list and put it in the Courier out front.''

''You'll be gone all afternoon?''

''Unless Dave is called away on an emergency and has to reschedule the operation.''

He seemed to give that considerable thought, and she wished for an insight into whatever was ticking over in his mind. Especially when she glimpsed a hint of wickedness around the edges of his quick smile. ''And picking up a few things for me won't be any trouble?''

''None at all.''

Despite an unsettling sense of *what-have-I-done?* she smiled brightly, turned and made it halfway down the breezeway before he called out to her.

''Tamara.''

T.C. closed her eyes, which was a big mistake. Without vision, the impact of his voice drawling her name intensified about a thousand times as it curled around her senses. Slowly she turned to face him.

''About our unfinished business...''

Her gaze was drawn to the source of those softly spoken words, to the mouth that had moved with such sure sensuality over hers. Her lips tingled just thinking about it. Was that the business he meant? She shook her head slightly, dismissing the notion, but only until Nick spoke again.

"We *will* get back to it," he assured her. "Later."

Nick had just finished washing an afternoon's hard labor from his body when he heard the rattle of a vehicle crossing the grid into the house-yard. A silver flash sped past the window, and his pulse did a surprising little snap to attention.

Ignoring his body's response, he leaned in close to the shower-fogged mirror, rasped a hand over his six-o'clock shadow and reached for his razor as the front door slammed. The noise reverberated through every timber beam in the low sprawling house, setting the long bank of picture windows rattling.

Nick winced.

She sounded about as mad as he figured she should be, considering the shopping list he'd left on her dash. Possibly over the top—no, *definitely* over the top—but unavoidable. It had ensured that she would be gone long enough even if the veterinary operation didn't go ahead. Long enough for him to get his plans back in order.

As he carefully maneuvered his razor through the dip in his chin, he wondered how long her snit would last and how long it would take him to cajole her out of it. The notion set up a powerful thrum of anticipation. She could play tough and indifferent all she liked, but that kiss had given her away. He hitched a towel around his hips and headed into his bedroom to dress, his smile ripe with expectation.

The sharp tap of her boot heels on the slate floor must have masked his arrival, so Nick leaned back against a kitchen bench and watched her crisscross the room, tossing packages into the fridge, then the pantry, muttering to herself most of the while. She turned and took several more strides before spotting him. Her gaze flicked from his face to his fingers, which were still busy fastening shirt buttons. Her stride faltered.

"Oh. You *are* here."

"Sorry I couldn't help you in with this stuff." He gestured at the grocery bags stacked on the island. "You caught me just out of the shower, and I figured you'd prefer if I put some clothes on. Right?"

Her gaze followed his hands as he tucked his shirt into his jeans. "Yes…um…right." Then, with a mental snap to attention that was almost audible, she swung back to the bench and buried her head in a grocery bag. "You could help me put this away instead of taking up space."

"I could. But then I wouldn't have the pleasure of watching you."

She rolled her eyes, clamped her teeth shut and continued stashing groceries.

It hadn't been a line—well, not entirely. The simmering temper suited her almost as well as the sweet-fitting jeans. There wasn't a lot to her top, so when she delved into the next bag it rode up her back to bare an enticing sliver of skin. He imagined sliding his hands over the silky warmth of her skin and laying his lips against her smooth golden nape.

As if his thoughts had been transmitted telepathically, she jumped sideways to put more space between them…and bumped her hipbone against a doorknob.

His attention was diverted by the hand rubbing her hipbone. It was the hand she'd injured earlier. "How is your thumb?"

"I'll live," she replied, with an abrupt little shrug.

"Did you see a doctor?"

"It's a scratch, for goodness' sake. Get over it." She tugged a tattered piece of paper from her pocket. Nick recognized his shopping list. "I managed to find most of this stuff, *eventually,* but I had no idea what this—" she stabbed a finger at his scrawled handwriting "—this hieroglyphic was supposed to be. Some sort of schnapps." She delved into the last bag and slapped a bottle down on the counter. "This is the best I could do."

"Is it butterscotch?"

"Does it matter?" she spluttered, eyes wide and incredulous.

Nick rubbed his chin as if giving the matter deep thought. Of course it didn't matter. He'd added it to the list while still savoring the impact of that rich, sweet, heady kiss—a kiss with a kick at the end that had left him breathless. Exactly like butterscotch schnapps.

"Oh, for goodness' sake! When I offered to shop for you I was thinking basics, not exotic liqueurs and fresh pasta and bloody Atlantic salmon. Riddells Crossing doesn't exactly cater to gourmet tastes." She snapped the last bag shut, crumpled it into a tight ball and strode over to the bin.

He could actually feel the hot vibes of her anger blazing across the space between them, but he couldn't help stoking the fire. "In my experience, shopping *improves* a woman's temperament," he said, tongue firmly in cheek. "Makes her amenable."

She spun around, eyes spitting green fire. "Amenable to do what? Cook for you?"

"Some do," he drawled. "Others just skip that step and head straight for the dessert tray."

"I'm sure *they* do. Me, I've never had much of a sweet tooth."

Nick laughed out loud. She was about as thorny as a full-grown prickly pear, yet that didn't seem to matter. He couldn't remember the last time he had felt so thoroughly entertained.

"I'm all done here, so I'll leave you to it," she said.

With a little jolt of alarm, Nick straightened off the bench. She couldn't be leaving—not without giving him a chance at some heavy-duty cajoling.

"But I haven't thanked you for doing the shopping." He moved closer, trapping her in the right angle where two benches met. He leaned nearer still, until he could reach around her to snag a bottle of wine from the bench top.

"Oh," she said, as if she had expected something else from his proximity. She moistened her parted lips. "I really have to go. My own groceries are in the car. They'll be getting hot."

"Really? I didn't think it was that hot. Are you hot, Tamara?"

She shook her head.

Liar.

The heat softened the brilliance of her eyes and flushed her cheeks and throat. Nick focused on the rapid pulse beating in the hollow of her throat, and the need to touch his lips to that spot, to taste her heat, gripped him suddenly and intensely.

Cool it, he told himself. Despite the heat sizzling between them, instinct told him she wasn't ready for hot and heavy. With a wry half smile, he brushed the backs of his fingers across her throat. She swallowed convulsively and almost climbed backward onto the bench.

"Please, don't touch me," she breathed, eyes wide and panicky.

"You didn't mind earlier, down at the stables."

"That was a mistake. I was upset with the accident and—" she took a deep breath that trembled "—it won't happen again."

"Now that would be a pity."

"Oh, puh-lease! There's no need to patronize me."

"I'm not. I enjoyed kissing you. I absolutely want to kiss you again." He regarded her through narrowed eyes. "The enjoyment seemed mutual."

She looked away. "As far as kisses go, it was okay, but I'm not interested in taking this any further."

For a second Nick thought about pushing it, about proving that he kissed—*they* kissed—better than okay. Slowly he lifted a hand toward her face, but her swift intake of breath, the wide frantic eyes, made him pause. She was scared. Scared of letting him close? Scared of her own response? Scared of the powerful chemistry between them?

It didn't matter which.

He wanted her leaning into him, meeting him halfway, as she'd done at the stables. He didn't care to analyze why, so he simply moved away.

Even after his retreat, T.C.'s heart continued to hammer against her rib cage. Feeling weak and hot and breathless, she lifted an absent hand to her throat, to where she swore the brush of his hand had blistered a trail right through her skin. She gazed longingly at the door. If only her weak, trembling legs could carry her there. She shifted her weight from one foot to the other and decided to give them another minute before trying them out.

"I think it's time we had that talk, Tamara." With an expert twist of his wrist, he decorked the wine, then laid the corkscrew on the bench.

T.C. shifted her weight again. Left foot, right foot. Right foot, left foot. Her strength seemed to be returning. She should leave.

Except her gaze was drawn to Nick as he poured two measures of Shiraz. He picked one up, twirling the glass in his long fingers so the liquid shimmered ruby-red in the light. He lifted it to his lips, took more than a sip, and a shiver of longing vibrated through her body.

God help her, she wanted to taste that wine on his lips. On his tongue.

Her gaze darted to the door. She had to leave before she did something stupid, like drinking the wine he'd obviously poured for her. With alcohol dulling her defenses it would be too easy to let him touch her again, to kiss her again, to turn her to mush with less than a casual fingertip. By purring her name, damn his too sexy, overconfident hide.

The sudden flash of temper fortified her, and her legs held her weight when she stood up straight. "I'm going now."

"You don't want to discuss this partnership problem?"

"Of course I do."

"Then how about you take the wine into the front room," he suggested smoothly, "while I throw a couple of steaks on the grill?"

"No." She shook her head emphatically. No way could she eat with him, drink with him, and concentrate on business. "I can't stay."

"Can't or won't?"

"Actually I'm going out." Dave *had* asked her to stay for dinner. She had declined, but it seemed like the perfect time to change her mind. She cleared her throat. "I have a dinner date."

His glass paused midway to his mouth. "With your vet friend?"

"How did you know that?"

"Lucky guess."

T.C. considered his bland expression, the small movement of his hand that caused the wine to circle his glass in measured motion, and she knew luck had nothing to do with that guess. Indignation washed through her, hot and fierce. "Do I take it you spent the afternoon grilling Jason?"

"We talked some."

"And Dave's name just happened to crop up?"

"We were discussing your nuisance calls," he said evenly. "I asked Jason about ex-boyfriends, and the vet's name came up."

"Dave is not an ex-boyfriend."

"Do you mean not an ex, or not a boyfriend?"

T.C. ignored that. "You had no right to quiz Jase about my friends," she said stiffly, although she could have used the singular form, such was the sad state of her social life. "There is no logical reason for the calls. Like I said before, it's most likely kids mucking about."

"If that's the case, they will stop. I ordered a silent number, and it's already in place." He pulled a piece of note paper from his pocket. "Don't give it out to anyone you wouldn't trust with your life. Okay?"

As she took in his sober expression and his strong bold print on the note, T.C. felt something she hadn't felt in a long time. She couldn't put a name to it, but it had to do with someone watching out for her, and at that moment it seemed as scarily seductive as the soft touch of his lips. She grabbed the note and backed up, half afraid she might do something crazy—like leaning into his strength.

"Thank you." She swallowed, slid both hands along with the note into her back pockets. "That's something I should have done. I don't know why I didn't think of it."

"Perhaps you've had too much else to think about."

Perhaps. That certainly sounded better than the alternative that sprang to her mind. She'd done nothing because she didn't want to admit she felt scared and threatened, because she didn't want to appear weak. How stupid would *that* sound if she tried to explain?

"So, what else did you and Jason talk about?" she asked to change the subject.

"Mostly about the horses, the stable routine. He's a good kid. You did well choosing him."

"He was Joe's choice, actually."

His eyes narrowed. "I sense there's a story here."

"Not really. His mother used to do some casual work here as a housekeeper before her husband died. Jase got into a bit of trouble. Bad company, not enough to occupy himself. Joe gave him a chance, and he turned out to be a natural."

"He says he learned it all from you—that you're the natural."

T.C. laughed self-consciously. "I told you I was good at my job."

"Yeah, you did."

He was watching her with serious eyes and the smallest hint of a smile on his beautiful lips, and her heart slammed hard against her ribs. Oh, help! She couldn't think of a thing to say. Couldn't move.

"You know, I really enjoyed myself this afternoon. I'd forgotten that elementally satisfying thing about manual labor, getting dirty and sweaty for a purpose."

"You helped Jase clean out the yard?"

He laughed, probably at the expression on her face. "No need to sound so shocked. With two of us, we got it done in less than half the time."

"So what did you do with all that time you saved?"

His pause was infinitesimal—just long enough for T.C. to realize she wasn't going to like what came next. "We shifted you back into the house."

"You shifted me…? You moved my things?" She pictured his hands on her clothes, her underwear, and felt both hot and cold at once. She sucked in a long breath, tried to summon some indignation. Unfortunately, all she could summon was a wishy-washy, "I wish you hadn't done that."

"I told you last night you were moving. Jase agreed it'd be easier if we presented it as a fait accompli."

"Jase wouldn't know a fait accompli if it bit him on the butt!"

His laughter was quick and unexpected and, like everything else about Nick Corelli, infectious. T.C. couldn't help responding, couldn't stop herself from grinning back at him. With a slow shake of his head, he caught her gaze, arched that one brow and said, "Damn, but you are a surprising woman. I thought you'd be going for my throat by now."

Her gaze skidded to the throat in question, and she felt that same hot-cold, heart-slamming response. How surprised would he be if she went for this throat with her lips and her tongue and her teeth? She swallowed the heat, the thought, the incredible temptation, and looked away. "I should be mad at you. I suspect, after I've stewed on it a while, I *will* be mad at you. I hate people touching my things."

"Yeah, you have a right to be angry," he said slowly. Then, "How long d'you usually stew on these things?"

Huh? She looked up, blinking, caught that hint of wickedness on his lips.

"I'm wondering if I should lock my door tonight...."

T.C. blinked again.

"I'd hate to be attacked in my sleep with something else from your toy arsenal."

"I don't have an arsenal. Jase's cousin left that cap gun when he was here one day. I found it out back and put it in the tack room and forgot about it until the other night." And why am I bothering to explain? He's packed all my things. He knows exactly what I own and don't own.

"So I can sleep soundly tonight?"

Oh great! All night she would be imagining Nick behind an *un*locked door, Nick sleeping soundly with his arms wrapped around his pillow, his tanned back exposed by the low-riding covers....

Brrriiiinnnngggg!

The first buzz of the phone resounded through T.C.'s bones. She would have sworn her feet literally left the ground, and her gaze, wide and panicked, flew to Nick's before she could censure herself. And as he reached for the cordless on the bench, his eyes told her exactly what she wanted to hear. *Relax. You're not on your own here. I've got this.*

"Yeah?" he barked into the receiver. Then the expression in his eyes, still focused intently on hers, softened. So did his voice when he said, "Lissa, honey, how's things?"

A slow smile spread across his face as he listened to *Lissa, honey's* long-winded reply. T.C. noticed his whole body relax, and as if there had been some weird energy transferal, her own tension compounded until she couldn't stand still.

She mouthed "I'll be going now" and gestured to the door. With one hand over the mouthpiece, Nick called, "Hang on a minute—I want to talk to you," but she kept on moving. She didn't stop until she'd slammed the door on the voice and the eyes that demanded she stay, even while some other woman, a woman trusted enough to have their new unlisted number, hung on the end of the telephone.

Nick, honey, I don't think so!

"You gonna take that job over in the west now?" Big Will, who single-handedly ran the only licensed premises in Riddells Crossing, slid T.C. the beer she had ordered and the question she had not been expecting in one smooth motion.

"Did I miss something?" T.C. shook her head, not understanding where Will was coming from or, for that matter going to, with his opening gambit.

"Now the son and heir's finally shown up, are you gonna take that job you were offered?"

"Ah, so Jase has been in here already tonight."

"You got it." Will grinned. "Didn't stay long. Red's here."

T.C. scanned the bar and found Red Wilmot in the far corner, lounging against the silent jukebox. He had recently returned home from a lengthy stay in juvenile detention, and there was something about his cocky stance and sneering face that had her quickly turning away before he caught her looking. "Do you suppose he's learned his lesson?"

"I know Jase has, thanks to you and Joe."

"Jase is a good kid. Red was a bad influence, that's all."

"You could have done us all a favor and brought this Corelli bloke in with you." The loud, intrusive voice came from one of the tables to her right. Judy Meicklejohn, T.C. decided without turning around.

"She's going to dinner with Dave," someone informed Judy. "She could hardly bring another bloke along."

"No kidding? I didn't know you and Dave were playing kissy-kissy."

"We're not," T.C. replied. "We're just friends."

When someone, probably Judy, made scoffing noises, T.C. shifted uncomfortably on her stool. She had told Nick she had a dinner date with Dave. She hadn't bothered telling *him* they were just friends. And why is that, Tamara Cole? she asked herself. Because you wanted to scare him off, or because you wanted him to think another man found you desirable?

"What's the story, T.C.?" Will interrupted her thoughts with another of his questions-from-nowhere.

"Which story would that be?"

"Joe's son from New York," Rory Meicklejohn interjected. "Is he a big hotshot?"

"Or, more to the point—is he big and is he hot?" T.C. didn't recognize that female voice, and because her face had turned hot, she didn't turn around to see who had made them all hoot with laughter.

"Jase says he's cool."

"Which doesn't mean he can't be hot. Come on, T.C., spill it. What's he like?"

A good question. "He only arrived last night, so it's hard to say," she replied carefully.

"You think he'll keep the place?"

"Why would a city slicker like him want a place out here?" Judy scoffed.

"Joe wanted a place out here."

"That's different. He *bought* the place."

"This geezer might like it here, too."

T.C. shut her ears to the speculation that flowed back and forth across the bar. She was still stuck on the "What's he like?" question and discovering that she might have misjudged him a teensy bit. Today she had discovered a real man beneath the smooth talker. That man had tended to her injury with a gentle efficiency, had helped Jase shovel muck for half the afternoon, and had worried enough about her security and comfort to move her back into the house *and* to change the phone number.

And which man changed your perception of how a kiss should be, Tamara Cole? Was that the real man or the smooth talker?

T.C. frowned into her beer and hoped it was the smooth talker, the one she'd left smiling for *Lissa, honey*. The one who had tricked her into shopping for him, who teased her in the kitchen with his soft touches and smarmy lines. Yes, she decided, with a reinforcing nod, the kiss had to be Mr. Smooth Talker.

Because if it was the real man, she was in big, big trouble.

Five

"**A**nyone in particular you're trying not to wake?"

The amused question startled T.C. into dropping the boots she'd been carrying, and she jerked her head around so sharply something pulled in her neck.

Oh, great! Whiplash is exactly what I need.

She lifted a hand to rub at her stiff neck and glared at the man responsible. Propped in the doorway to the office, a mug in one hand and a sheaf of papers in the other, he looked far too awake for five-thirty in the morning.

"You want me to do that for you?" His velvet-coated drawl stroked her sleepy senses to immediate complete wakefulness; the thought of his strong, supple hands on her neck sent them into hyperactivity.

No!

No more touching. Last night she had decided that the best way to defuse the Nick-factor was to avoid all nonbusiness-related situations.

"I didn't expect you to be up this early," she admitted.

"My body clock's taking a while to adjust. I was awake before three, but then I crashed at ten."

So there had been no need to stay out late. Damn, she wished she had known that.

"Did you enjoy your evening?"

"Very much." Which wasn't so much a lie as a relative truth. When Dave had finally arrived after a difficult emergency procedure, they'd ditched the restaurant in favor of takeout. Dave fell asleep halfway through the combination of chow mein and cop show. T.C. had finished the food, channel-surfed into the early hours and worked on convincing herself that she preferred comfortable and stress-free to unpredictable and edgy. Like, say, the Shiraz-and-steaks-with-Nick alternative she had turned down.

Nick straightened away from the door frame and waved his mug. "Coffee's not long made."

Filling her nostrils with the strong fresh aroma tested her resolve, but she shook her head. "Thanks, but I'll just grab some juice and keep going."

She retrieved her boots and headed for the kitchen, remembering at the last minute to dispense with the sneaking.

"Do you always start this early?" he asked from close behind.

T.C. almost dropped her boots again. "Usually." As she grabbed a glass and swung across to open the fridge, she felt the warmth of his lazy inspection all the way to her toes.

"Sure you don't want coffee?"

Leaning further into the refrigerator's cooling depths, she mumbled a negative reply and tried to recall what she was looking for. When she slammed the door shut in exasperation, she found him still watching her, and the refrigerator's chilling effect immediately evaporated.

With a barely articulate "See you later" she dispensed

with the glass, snatched an apple from the fruit bowl and bolted.

"Is that breakfast?" he asked as he followed her to the back door.

"I don't like to eat early," she lied. "I catch up later, after fast work."

"Fast work happens to be my specialty."

With a mental eye-roll, she explained how her version of fast work referred to exercising the horses fast, in full race harness, as opposed to their slow work or jog days. "Jase and I usually do fast work first thing."

"Jase will be a little late today, but I'll—"

"What do you mean, a little late?"

"Ten. Eleven." He shrugged as if it didn't matter either way.

"It would have been nice to know this."

"I tried to tell you last night, but you bolted before I could finish."

True, but that didn't make it any easier to digest. "Please check with me before you go giving him any more time off," she said stiffly.

"Sure." His drawl sounded smoothly agreeable, but as she bent to pull on her boots, T.C. caught a coolness in his eyes. "In case you're interested in why, his mother wants him to take her to the cemetery."

The cemetery. T.C. closed her eyes as a cold wave of remorse crashed over her. It was the anniversary of Jase's father's death in a work accident, and she should have remembered. *She* should have given Jase the time off. He should have asked *her*.

As she followed Nick out into the predawn chill, her legs felt stiff and uncooperative, as if in physical response to her mental wretchedness. Jase had worked with her for more than two years, his mother Cheryl for longer, yet he hadn't come to her.

Had she become so unapproachable? So closed that he would prefer to ask a stranger?

She glanced at the stranger walking beside her, recalled his instant rapport with Jason, and her own bitter response. Shame burned through her, stopping her in her tracks.

"I wish I'd known—I would have taken them out there myself, or at least given Jase the day off."

"He only took a couple of hours because I insisted."

"I'm such a hard boss?"

"He thought he'd be letting you down."

She closed her eyes briefly, struggled against the savage lash of emotion, didn't know what to say. She didn't deserve such loyalty—lately, she had done nothing to deserve it.

"Come on. The sooner we get started, the sooner we get to eat breakfast."

T.C. didn't move. She needed alone; she needed composure. The last thing she needed was Nick's unsettling presence. "There's no need for you to do this."

"Yes, there is. I promised Jase."

She shook her head. "I don't have time to teach you what I want done. I'll be quicker on my own."

He stared down at her for a minute that seemed like ten. "It doesn't hurt to accept help, Tamara."

"I would accept your help—if it *was* a help."

He let out his breath in sharp exasperation and looked off into the distance. "We need to resolve this partnership bind. D'you suppose you can fit that into your busy schedule?"

His voice held all the warmth of a winter southerly, and it cut through T.C. just as surely. His approval didn't matter, she told herself, but the appointment did. "This afternoon? After I finish work?"

"Perfect." With that he turned on his heel and strode back the way they had come. T.C. held her breath until he disappeared beyond the bank of melaleucas lining the house-yard. He was gone, out of her hair for the best part of the day. She couldn't have planned it any better.

So why did she feel such an intense desire to call him back?

It took Nick all morning to deal with the paperwork Melissa had e-mailed, and finishing it was about the only enjoyable part of the exercise—that and knowing she would now get off his case.

His partner could be a real pain in the butt…when she wasn't being brilliant. With a wry grimace, he recalled the set down she'd given him yesterday when, in her words, she finally got him to answer the bloody phone. Dealing with her from this far away had its advantages. Like he could call her *Lissa, honey* without getting swatted around the ears. She hated endearments almost as much as she hated the way he abbreviated her name.

So why had he answered the phone that way? To get up her nose, or because he wanted to prove a point to Tamara?

The point being?

That he didn't give a flying fig about her decision to eat with the on-again off-again boyfriend. That he would be just fine on his own, thanks for asking.

With an impatient shove, he propelled his chair away from the desk and let it swing in a half circle. He stretched his arms high, cracked his knuckles and ignored the temptation to look out the window. He would not check up on her, even under the guise of seeing if Jason had arrived yet.

She had made it clear she didn't want his help. She'd made it clear she didn't want anything from him, and although she appealed to him on many levels—the courage she'd shown in confronting him that first night, her fierce loyalty to Joe, the incredibly stimulating touch of her hand...oh, and the way she kissed—she was way too prickly, too complex.

A thousand headaches in the making.

Just as soon as he had made a partnership-breaking deal, he would be on the first plane back to his life—the life he had made for himself. With a resolute nod he turned back to the desk and the box-file George had handed him before he walked out of their meeting.

"Crunch time, Niccolo," he muttered as his glance slid over the solicitor's label: Estate Of The Late Joe Corelli. Ignoring the sudden tightness in his chest, he slipped on his reading glasses and extracted the first wad of papers.

It was almost seven before T.C. forced herself to sit down in the living room—much later than she had anticipated, but by the time Jason had arrived that morning she had been way behind schedule. She had wanted to talk to him but couldn't find the words, and that sat badly with her throughout the afternoon, so every small task had seemed to take twice as long. Then she had needed a good long shower, and if she tried hard enough she could even justify changing her clothes three times before deciding on her usual combination of jeans, tank top and flannel shirt.

She could justify all night long, but when it came down to it, she was a coward. This conversation with Nick would likely decide her future—whether she stayed in the place she had come to accept as home, or whether she would be forced to ring that Perth trainer and take the alternative he offered. Yet she feared she wasn't up to it. It surprised her that she had found the nerve to knock at the office door, to push it open a fraction, to inform Nick she would be in the living room. She hadn't waited for his reply; she hadn't even looked in. She had pulled the door shut and kept on walking.

Maybe her father had been right. Maybe she was a little girl playing in a man's world.

Before she could sink into that mire of self-pity, Nick strolled into the room. Watching him move, so loose limbed and full of masculine grace, had the usual effect. Her pulse thudded, the air in her lungs turned hot and thick, and the soft denim of her much-washed jeans felt harsh against her skin, her buttoned cuffs too tight for her wrists.

"This is for you," he said without preliminary. "I think you should read it before we talk."

Read what? She blinked, noticed the guarded expression on his face before she noticed the envelope in his hand. The warm flush under her skin prickled with a strong sense of déjà vu.

Another letter from the grave.

She needed to run her tongue twice around her dry mouth before she could speak. "Where did this come from?"

"It was in the papers George gave me. I only went through them this afternoon."

"What do you mean...in the papers? Was it hidden? Didn't anyone know it was there?"

"I don't know. I'm sorry, but that's the truth." When she didn't take the envelope, he dropped it in her lap. "I'll leave you to read it in peace. Then we'll talk."

He left abruptly, leaving T.C. staring at the envelope until Joe's big boldly printed *T.C.* blurred into her father's spidery version. She sat up straight and shook her head.

"What is wrong with you? Why don't you just open it?"

There was no reason not to. This time there would be no bitter recriminations, no reminders of what a disappointment she had been as a daughter...or because she'd been a daughter. No terse words informing her that the family home, the stables and all the horses, had been left to an uncle she barely knew.

She squeezed her eyes tightly closed, as if that might

contain the hurt, stop it spreading from the deep-seated knot in her heart, and with a deep, shuddery breath she ripped into the envelope. Her trembling hands smoothed out the single sheet of vellum. Only then was she capable of opening her eyes.

Nick figured she needed privacy, and he wanted to try to reach George one last time. Not that talking to him would do any good—he would simply deny any knowledge of the letter. He had been obstructive from the get-go, but that was no surprise.

That was George.

Still, he jabbed out part of the number he'd dialed enough times in the past hours to know by heart, but then he pictured Tamara staring at the envelope, her face as pale as if Joe himself had appeared before her. With a harsh curse, he jammed down the receiver and went looking for her.

He found her sitting on the verandah steps, framed by the pale light cast through a foyer window. The dog clutched in her arms inspected Nick with solemn eyes, but Tamara didn't look up, and he knew she'd been crying.

Hell!

She sat hunched forward, body language screaming *keep away,* but whispering *hold me.* With a sense of fatalism riding him hard, he sat down next to her, close enough to feel her stiffen defensively.

"My shoulder's here if you need something to cry on," he offered.

"I'm not crying." She swiped the back of one hand across her eyes.

"It's okay. I don't mind a wet shoulder."

"It's not okay. Crying is weak and foolish and female."

Nick snorted. "Anyone who's tried to sneak into your stables in the middle of the night knows you're not weak. Definitely female, but never weak."

"You forgot foolish."

Nick smiled at her churlishness. "Yeah, well, some might consider what you did foolish. Others would call it brave."

When her tense posture relaxed fractionally, he felt a disproportionate degree of satisfaction. "You want to talk about what Joe had to say?"

"What did he tell you?" she asked carefully.

Nick shook his head, not understanding.

"In your letter... He did leave you a letter?"

"No."

She turned toward him slightly, enough that he could see the frown creasing her brow. "You're his son—you're family. Why would he write to me and not you?"

"Perhaps you were closer to him than any of his family."

She made a disbelieving little noise, then shifted restlessly, as if even considering that notion didn't sit well with her. "The first years I worked here, I didn't know him at all," she said softly. "He didn't stay over much, just came for a day whenever he could, rang maybe once a week. After his wife died, he started staying weekends, occasionally longer. I can almost see why people might have thought we were..." She cleared her throat. "It was only this last six months that he stayed most of the time."

"Did he know he was...?"

Dying.

The unsaid word hung heavily between them. To Nick, the air felt morbidly thick. That was why breathing was so damn difficult.

"I don't know," she replied in that same slow, considering voice. "He said nothing to me. I don't think anyone knew how sick he was."

No one had said a word, not to him at any rate. Big surprise! He had returned from a month in Alaska to a coldly formal solicitor's letter. The memory was as keen as the day he slit the seal on that innocuous looking envelope.

"I didn't know," he said, his voice so gruff he barely recognized it as his own. "I didn't know anything until it was all over."

When she placed her hand on his arm, Nick didn't shake it off. This time he accepted the firm, warm contact. He accepted it, and he waited for some cloying words of sympathy to break the peculiar bond he felt with this woman he barely knew, but who knew exactly how to touch him.

She surprised him by saying nothing.

They sat like that for a long time, their silence comfortable and comforting. Then her hand moved on his forearm. It was simply a shift in pressure, hardly a caress, yet it aroused his senses in a heartbeat. The sweet fragrance of some flowering shrub filled his nostrils, the hoot of an owl sounded preternaturally loud on the still night air, and she drifted closer, her eyes luminous in the ambient light.

His lips were only a whisper away when Ug bounded to life in her lap. T.C. turned her head sharply, and his lips grazed across her cheek. She laughed awkwardly, then sprang to her feet, dusting the backside of her jeans. "I have to go double-rug the horses. The nights are getting cold."

Before he could reply, she was steaming off down the path. He had to raise his voice to be sure it would reach her. "How are we ever going to organize anything if you keep running away?"

She slowed, her dark silhouette wavering against the silvery outline of the stable block. "I have to rug up," she insisted.

"We have to discuss our partnership."

She lifted a hand and rubbed it through her tumbled locks, and he heard her faint, frustrated sigh. "Then why don't you come help me?"

* * *

T.C. ran a hand under Monte's rug, then stepped back while Nick threw a second, heavier, blanket over the top. Accepting his help hadn't hurt, and he had been right on another account. She had to stop running away. They had to discuss how they would handle this partnership. Before she could change her mind or find another excuse to procrastinate, she blurted, "My half share in Yarra Park is Joe's idea of insurance."

Nick clicked the leg straps in place without missing a beat. "Insurance against...?"

"Selling up. Joe seemed to think you might not even consider keeping the place." She took a deep breath, found it rich with straw and horse and all things important. "Was he right?"

"Yes."

"You can't do that without my agreement. That's why Joe left me half." It was a sound reason, one she understood. She wished it was the only reason Joe had given.

Nick's blue gaze narrowed intently on hers as he approached. "I could if I bought you out."

"There isn't any offer I will accept."

He paused in front of her, eyebrows raised. "No?"

"No!" She stood her ground, lifting her chin defiantly.

"What if I offered you enough to start your own stables?"

"Money doesn't tempt me."

He smiled as she let him out of the box—a practiced smile that perfectly matched the calculating gleam in his eyes. So this was Nick the Trader, the financial whiz who effortlessly raked in the millions. Funny, but this version of Nick didn't scare her at all. *This* Nick wouldn't send her running.

"What if I threw in your pick of the horses?" he asked, his tone as slick and smooth as molasses. "Take any six you fancy."

"What if I told you I wouldn't take a million dollars and all the horses on this place?"

"I'd say you were bluffing...or crazy."

"This isn't about money, Nick. This place has never been about money."

"No?"

She looked him right in the eye, her message direct and sincere. "Joe built it from nothing. He must have looked at fifty parcels of land before he found the one that felt right. It had nothing to do with the price tag and everything to do with his heart. That's why it is so special."

And that was why she had to do all she could to uphold Joe's wishes—not only because she owed him, but because she understood how much it meant to him. She leaned closer to Nick, willing him to do more than listen. Needing him to *hear* her.

"This is no consolation prize, Nick. This place mattered more to Joe than anything. He loved Yarra Park, and he doesn't want it sold. You have to understand what it meant to him."

A fierce passion burned deep in her eyes. Hell, from this close Nick could practically feel her whole body resonating with it. What would it be like to taste that white-hot intensity? How would it feel to be buried deep inside it, to be wrapped in all that passion? He lifted a hand and placed it against the side of her neck, felt the leap of her pulse and the answering drum of his own.

"*You* understand. Maybe I should sign my half over to you," he murmured, watching her lips, thinking about them under his.

"I hope you're joking!"

She pulled back abruptly, his hand fell away, and he was left staring into her wide eyes. She was clearly appalled...and probably not only by his offer. The fact that he was putting a move on her in the middle of this conversation appalled *him*.

With a mental grimace, he leaned back against the door, shoved his hands into his pockets and considered her question. Was he joking about giving his half away? "He should have left you the whole caboodle. I have no interest in horses, and my home's in New York."

"Your home's been at least ten places in the last ten years," she countered hotly. Then, as if realizing she had given too much away, she bit her lip and looked away. A slow color suffused her face. "Not that anyone's keeping count."

Nick leaned more heavily against the stable door. He felt weird, off-balance, as he considered what she had let slip—not the one instance, but the whole picture. Joe talking about him, about his life, to this stranger who didn't feel like a stranger. And Joe singling him out, gifting him with his most precious asset. "Joe talked a lot, huh?"

She scuffed her foot against the concrete, shrugged one shoulder. "When he came up here he did. I guess he felt he could tell me things his family didn't want to hear."

"If it was about me, they definitely wouldn't have wanted to hear."

"You don't exactly get along with your brother and sisters, do you?"

It was Nick's turn to shrug. He shouldn't have said anything. He shouldn't have felt compelled to talk to her about something so personal, something he never talked about. "We've gotten off subject."

"Yes, we have." She fixed him with a straight look. "You don't have to sell up, you know. It's not like you need the money."

"What do you suggest we do?"

"Nothing. You go back to New York, and I continue to manage Yarra Park the way I've been doing."

Agreeing should have been a cinch. She was right—he didn't need the money—and he realized that despite only knowing her two days, he trusted her. Yet there was something about the way she held herself, as if on hearing his *Why not?* she would burst into a great whoop of delight.

"Well?" she asked, the one short word jammed full of impatient expectancy.

"Okay," he drawled, but when relief spread across her face with the startling brilliance of a perfect sunrise, some perverse part of his nature dug its heels in. "I'll consider it," he heard himself saying. "In the meantime, I'd like to help out. If I learn how things work it will make it easier to communicate after I leave."

Her sunrise smile dimmed about sixty degrees. "What do you mean? Aren't you going back to New York?"

"Not immediately. I prefer to do my considering on site."

"But what about your business?"

"I'll need to put in a couple of extra lines, but I can manage from anywhere with a modem and a telephone. That's the beauty of my business."

She swallowed, cleared her throat. "For how long?"

"As long as it takes."

A whole gamut of emotions flitted across her expressive face. Shock, horror, dread. And beneath them all burned the unasked question.

As long as it takes to do what?

To assess her competence as a stable manager, her integrity as a business partner?

Or for her to stop running?

Nick wasn't sure *he* knew the answer. An hour ago he had been ready to pack his bags; half an hour later he had sat with her hand on his arm feeling as if he never wanted to move, ever again. Ten minutes ago he had been contemplating hot, immediate sex against a stable wall.

Now, as he stared down at her, those thoughts of open-mouthed kisses and soft yielding flesh must have shown, for a panicky kind of awareness turned her skin soft and rosy. She took a step back and blurted, "I'm not sleeping with you."

"Well, I'm glad we cleared the air on that issue." And as if the air really had been cleared, he smiled negligently and arched a brow. "But wouldn't it have been polite to wait until you were asked?"

Six

Somewhere shy of midnight, T.C. gave up all pretense of sleep, swung her legs out of bed and pressed a hand to her grumbling stomach. Food had been the last thing on her mind when she had turned and walked away through the silence that followed Nick's humiliating jibe.

Operating on automatic pilot, she had come straight to her room and paced a path in the carpet as she replayed the evening's events over and over again. Of course she kept returning to that dreadful moment when her fears flew heedlessly to her tongue.

I'm not sleeping with you.

How could she have said that? Sure, she had thought about it. Often. What red-blooded woman wouldn't fantasize about Nick Corelli in her bed? But she had gone and *said it*—to his face—and now she would have to deal with the mortifying fact that she had completely misinterpreted the intent behind his kiss and those touches. Quite likely he treated all women the same way. A little flirting, a lot of charm. She would do well to remember the kind of man he was, and *that* kind of man she could deal with. Her experience with Miles had taught her that much.

Dealing with the man who had sat beside her on the verandah steps was not so easy. How tempting it had been to take up his offer, to lean into his strength, to let go of everything dammed up inside. Years and years and years of pretending she could cope, that she needed no one. Worse—how could she deal with the memory of his anguish and her own fiercely intense need to comfort him? That moment when something foreign and unexpected and dangerous had flared in her heart, something that went way beyond physical desire.

How could she work in partnership with him?

How could she not, knowing this was the only way of repaying her debt to Joe?

With a heavy sigh, she pushed herself to her feet and followed her stomach to the kitchen. She didn't bother with artificial lights—the full moon was bright enough to cast well-defined shadows as she poured a mug of milk and searched the pantry for something filling that didn't need preparation, finding it in the last of a batch of double-choc muffins Cheryl had sent over the previous week. She recalled Jason's goofy grin as he handed her the container, and how she had made her usual halfhearted protest, "She shouldn't have," while the sinfully rich aroma of fresh baking seeped into her pores.

"That's what I said," Jase replied, "but she reckons you don't look after yourself properly."

A week ago the caring behind Cheryl's gesture had settled pleasurably somewhere deep inside. Tonight, as she took her supper into the living room, that same place churned with regret. These past months she had been too wrapped up in her own loss to spare a thought for Cheryl's pain as she relived the events of twelve months before.

It hadn't surprised anyone when she grieved long and

hard for her husband. They had shared a special closeness, the kind visitors immediately felt in the open warmth of their home. Watching the exchanged glances and casual touches, as if they communicated in some secret shorthand, had never failed to move T.C.

Sometimes she would lie awake through the loneliest hours and wonder what it might be like to experience such intimacy; other times she would sternly reprimand herself for yearning after the unattainable. Better to be strong and insular than dependent on another for your happiness.

"Can't sleep?"

She turned her head to see Nick standing in the archway leading to the hall. Her heart quickened instantly.

"The full moon always unsettles me." It wasn't exactly a lame excuse, but it had a definite limp.

He came into the room, all rumpled hair and bare chest and long naked legs. She looked away, swallowed a hot gulp. *Holy jiminy.* He was wearing nothing but shorts, and he was taking a seat at the other end of the sofa, less than an arm's length away.

He gestured toward the remains of her supper. "You should have come out for dinner. You can't live on snacks."

"That's what Cheryl says." She could feel warmth in her cheeks, everywhere on her skin, and was as thankful for the low light as for the subject. Anything to distract her overactive imagination. "I was thinking about her just now, her and Pete. I guess that's another reason why I couldn't sleep."

"You want to know why I couldn't sleep?"

He tilted his head, and the moonlight slanted across his face, highlighting the sharp plane between cheekbone and jaw, making him look a lot less laid-back, a lot more dangerous. Her heartbeat kicked up another notch.

"I guess you have a lot on your mind," she said. "I know I have."

When he turned more fully toward her it was tough not
to stare at all that bare skin, near impossible not to track
the pattern of dark hair across his broad chest and down
toward the low-riding waist of his shorts. Oh help, she had
to concentrate on something else. Not those long athlete's
legs…maybe his arms. One rested along the back of the
sofa, and as she took in the strong curve of his biceps and
the softer, almost vulnerable line of his underarm, the tug
of attraction was so powerful she could barely breathe. She
forced herself to look away. To breathe.

"I couldn't sleep because I was thinking about what you
said down at the stables, and my knee-jerk reaction."

There was no reason to expound; she knew exactly what
he was referring to.

I'm not sleeping with you.

"Is it because of your vet?"

"Dave?" She thought about taking the easy road, then
rejected it. It seemed like the time for honesty. "No.
Dave's a good friend. I wish it were more, but…" She
shrugged.

"No fire?"

"Not even a spark. Look, it was a bit previous of me
to assume…"

"To assume I want to get you into my bed?" Their eyes
met and held. Spark, fire, inferno. T.C. felt her whole body
combust. "It was a fair enough assumption."

It took a long time to assimilate that simple statement.
What did he mean? And did she really want to know?

"You have that scared look in your eyes again. Why is
that? The night we met, when you came after me with that
cap gun, I thought nothing would scare you."

The tips of his fingers touched her hair, and she recoiled
sharply, pulling her legs up under her in an unwittingly
defensive posture.

"What are you so afraid of?"

"I'm scared of how far out of my depth I am," she

said, the words tumbling out in a breathy rush. "I don't know what you want from me."

"I think you do know. I think that's what scares you."

His voice was as soft as the moonlight, as dark and alluring as the shadows. T.C. felt a shiver run through her. Not cold, but heat. "Casual sex isn't something I handle well," she breathed.

"You think this would be casual?"

Her startled gaze flew to his and was immediately trapped by his intent expression. Her breathing grew shallow; her pulse pounded like racing hoofbeats on summer-hard earth.

"I imagine nothing's ever casual with you," he said slowly.

"Yes, well, that's my problem. I take everything way too seriously."

"Funny, but that's exactly what I've been telling myself ever since I met you. That you're too serious and prickly and difficult."

How did he do it? How did he turn such an uncomplimentary description into flattery, just with a look?

"I don't know what to say to that."

"How about, 'I'm not usually this prickly but around you I'm on edge all the time. I can't sleep nights. I toss and turn until the sheets are as hot and twisted as the images in my mind'?"

A throttled sound rose from her throat. "I get your drift," she growled, shifting restlessly, feeling as hot and twisted as the images he painted. Needing to escape them but needing to set this straight. "I *am* attracted to you, physically, and there's been all this emotional drama drawing us together. The way we feel about Joe... But that's all this is. I mean, if it weren't for Joe, we would never have met. You are hardly the kind of guy I'd have bumped into at a friend's place. If you'd passed me on the street, you wouldn't have spared me a second glance."

"How do you know that?"

She rolled her eyes. "Believe me, I know. We don't live in the same world, Nick. We have nothing in common."

"Other than the fact that Joe tied us together."

Her eyes widened at his choice of words; then she quickly lowered her lids to hide her reaction. No way was she ever letting him know how closely she thought Joe wanted them tied.

"You want to know what I feel about this?" he asked.

She met his eyes with a heartfelt plea in hers. *Please, don't go there. Don't say it.* The deep breath she took seemed to shudder with tension. "I think it's best if we leave this where we were before. I'm not sleeping with you, and you're not asking."

"Best for who?" A hint of humor touched his mouth. "It sure doesn't feel like it's best for me."

And looking at him sitting there, so decadently beautiful—the bed-ruffled hair she yearned to smooth, the shadowed planes of his cheeks, that direct blue gaze—it didn't feel best for T.C., either. When she felt the temptation tingle through her nerve endings, she sat on her hands and bit down on her lip.

His last line, the delivery, the wicked glint in his eyes, called for a witty, teasing response, but she couldn't think of a thing. Better to change the subject.

"I've been thinking—" She had to stop, clear her throat, it was so husky. "I've been thinking about what I said earlier, about you going back to New York and me managing Yarra Park."

"Change your mind?"

"No." She shook her head emphatically. "But I don't think I was completely clear. I'm not comfortable with accepting this bequest."

"It's how Joe wanted it."

"Only in a de facto kind of way. It would have been

easier if he gave you all of Yarra Park with the proviso that you keep me on as manager.''

''You answered that one earlier. He didn't trust me not to sell up.''

''What if I gave you my half and we drew up an agreement that says you can't sell?''

''Hang on.'' Nick held up a hand. ''You won't take money for your half but you want to give it away? Am I missing something here?''

T.C. blew out a puff of frustration. ''Look, I don't want to own Yarra Park, I just want to live here, to work here, and the only money I want is wages. You don't want to live here, but surely owning the place doesn't bother you. Couldn't we come to some kind of agreement where we both get what we want?''

He didn't answer right away, and that gave her some hope. Then he shook his head. ''I don't think—''

''You don't have to think, you only have to agree.'' She leaned forward, imploring him to reconsider. ''Will you please think about it?''

He got to his feet and stalked to the window. For a long silent minute he stood there, his silhouette etched broad and strong by the frosted light, while T.C.'s whole being vibrated with a powerful longing that transcended the physical. She wanted to talk to him, *really* talk to him. She wanted to tell him all the reasons why she couldn't accept the bequest, yet she feared he wouldn't understand.

He turned to face her, his expression impossible to read in the tricky shadows. ''I have to be back in New York on the twenty-fifth. That gives me two weeks to think about this. How does that sound?''

About thirteen days too long.

He came closer and offered his hand, pulling her to her feet and not letting go. Suddenly the air seemed close with his body heat, redolent with his scent. She felt more than a little giddy and struggled not to lean on him for support, then struggled for something to ease the tension.

"Are we shaking on anything in particular?" she asked.

"Shaking?"

He looked down, seemed to consider her hand in his. She felt his grip tighten infinitesimally, and it felt as if something closed reflexively around her heart. Oh boy. Too much Nick at too close a distance. She tried to regain her hand and failed.

"How about we shake to mutual satisfaction?" he purred. Then he laughed in the same low, dark tone, probably at the confused heat in her expression. "You said we should both get what we want, and that sounds fine by me. Deal?"

T.C. blinked as he shook her hand; then she managed to tug her fingers free and back up until her knees hit the couch. If Nick hadn't been there, a solid anchor for her wildly flailing arms, she would have toppled right down, but once she'd regained her balance he stepped clear and yawned with a total lack of self-consciousness. "Seems like it might be worth giving sleep another try."

She managed to mumble something resembling *goodnight,* and he left as noiselessly as he had arrived, leaving her with three distinct impressions.

Number one—touching him was like absorbing his voice. Velvet over steel. Soft and harsh, darkness and light. Two—she didn't feel like she had shaken on anything resembling mutual satisfaction. Three—sleep would be a long time coming.

Nick wasn't sure why he had exercised such restraint during that moonlight meeting the previous night. The whole hour had been one painful exercise in self-restraint, and when she overbalanced and grabbed at his arms—hell, he'd been one narrow noble streak from following her

down onto that couch. From covering her head to foot,
skin against skin.

Noble streak? Huh!

He hadn't used that description for years, maybe a de-
cade. It was Joe who had introduced him to the term—
said it was unusual to find a kid with such a noble streak.
Given his background, the irony hadn't escaped Nick, nor
had the impact of the compliment, and now Joe had gone
and topped it.

He had left him his most precious asset. The ultimate
compliment. He felt humbled, honored and, to top it off,
mighty confused. Why would Joe single him out? Sure,
he'd accepted him into his family and done his best to be
fair, to treat him as one of his own children, but they both
knew he was only distant kith and kin. That was why
George was being such a pain in the rear.

Tamara would know. Even without the benefit of that
letter, she knew more about Joe's thinking in those last
months than anyone else. But would she tell him? That
was the killer question. He had never met a woman so
closed, so unwilling to let anything of herself out, so afraid
to let anything of herself go.

Man, but he wanted to know what went on in her head.

As if responding to the power of that thought, she came
walking into the kitchen. Stopped. A faint touch of color
traced her cheekbones as her gaze met his, then slid away.
Then she seemed to gather herself, to take a strengthening
breath, and she kept coming. Nick felt breathless himself.
He couldn't figure out why she affected him so immediately, so completely. As usual, she was dressed to make
as little of herself as possible, yet something about the way
she moved, the way she looked at him, was all woman.
Yep, she only had to lean into the fridge at that certain
angle to jump-start his engine.

"You want coffee?" he asked, hoping for once she
would surprise him and say "yes."

"Yes, please."

Nick didn't do a double take. After all, she had been one surprise after another from the moment they met.

"What are your plans for today?" she asked as she brought milk and cereal to the table.

"Might as well start as I aim to continue. Down at the barn."

Her eyes widened. "You're serious about learning how the stables run?"

"Yes, ma'am."

"We'll see how long you last on the end of a pitchfork, city slicker."

Nick smiled back. He liked the teasing warmth in her eyes. Very much. "I don't mind getting my boots dirty."

He watched her munch her way through a hearty helping of cereal before he spoke again. At least if she bolted he wouldn't feel responsible for another missed meal.

"You mind if I ask you something personal?"

She paused, coffee mug suspended halfway between table and mouth, her face all big-eyed suspicion. "That depends."

"I wondered why you needed this job so badly." What caused that emotional pounding she had hinted at. "You don't have to tell me. I'm just curious," he said easily, as if he hadn't spent sleepless hours pondering the many possibilities.

"You know what happened to the curious cat." Still teasing, although more warily this time. At least she hadn't walked away. Yet.

"Are you a local?"

"Our family had a small acreage about an hour's drive west of here," she said carefully. "I lived there till I was seventeen."

"Was that when your father died?"

She took a measured sip of her coffee. "That was two years later."

"Your mother?"

"She died when I was little. I barely remember her." She put her mug down with an abrupt click. "I don't know if you're really interested in my family history or if this is breakfast small talk, so I'll keep it brief. My father brought us up—my brother and me—which wasn't so bad, because we both happened to love horses and they were Dad's life. Jonno was killed when I was fifteen, and things went downhill from there. I stayed as long as I could, but when I got a decent job offer, I left."

"Sometimes leaving's best for everyone."

"Well, my father sure didn't think so." She swirled the remains of her coffee around the mug, a small sad smile on her lips. "Obviously he wasn't as forgiving as Joe."

"He was tough on you?"

"Yes, but he also taught me how to work and about self-discipline." She lifted her chin, defied him to take issue.

"Seems to me you're too hard on yourself. Maybe you needed someone to teach you about lightening up, having fun."

"I've tried that. It's overrated."

Nick wondered if that was what her father hadn't forgiven—not the leaving home, but what she had done in those years—and what his lack of forgiveness had meant to her. "What happened to your father's place?" he asked on a hunch.

She shrugged, but the gesture seemed awkward. And telling. "He left it to someone else."

A father gutted by the death of his son, a daughter who tried to fill the gap but felt she had failed, who maybe ran wild for a couple of years. And her bitter, tough, unforgiving father gives away her heritage.

It explained a lot about the woman sitting before him. Her self-contained strength, her vulnerability, how she worked her butt off, as if paying some sort of penance.

Her reluctance to accept what she thought she didn't deserve.

"And this is why you don't want to accept your part of Yarra Park?"

Determination hardened her expression. "It's not right. Joe's family should have it. I know how they must feel about this."

"Joe's family is getting plenty. Believe me, this is nothing like the situation between you and your father."

"But..."

"Accept it, Tamara. It's what Joe wanted."

"But you said you would consider taking my half."

"I said I'd think about it, and I will. Are you this stubborn about everything?" Man, he hoped not. He had less than two weeks to change her mind, and he didn't mean about the inheritance.

"Stubborn?" She pushed herself off her stool, a faint smile curving her lips. "As a mule, Joe used to say, but only about things that matter. Now, let's go find you a pitchfork."

The next five days rolled out smoothly enough, with Nick dividing his time between the stables and the office. Although he made no overt moves or provocative comments, tension simmered beneath the artificial surface of civility, despite her attempts to keep the mood light and easy. The flame had been turned down to pilot, but one quick flick of the switch would kindle the inferno she had felt that night in the moonlight.

Eight more days, she thought with a resigned sigh as she let herself into Star's stall. Could she keep a grip on her twitchy fingers that long?

She waited while the big mare went through her you-can't-catch-me routine, prancing from wall to wall with a succession of disdainful head tosses. Collaring her was a game of skill, patience and acquired knowledge. "Fin-

ished?'' she asked when the pirouettes ended abruptly.
Timing was everything in this game. With a nimble side-
step, she intercepted a further halfhearted attempt at a pass
and slipped the head collar into place.

"Ready for some work?" Star tossed her head with arrogant scorn, and T.C. laughed softly. "Silly question,
huh? You love to run."

As she smoothed her hand down the mare's neck, a
sense of contentment settled in the pit of her stomach. This
was why she had chosen this profession, for this simple,
elemental feeling. Stooping down, she felt the mare's near
foreleg, checking for heat in the tendon she had injured
the previous season.

"Looking good, girl." Satisfied with the inspection, she
straightened to find Star nodding her head as if in agreement. T.C. couldn't help but laugh. "You are so full of
yourself!"

The sound of her laughter brought Nick's grooming mitt
to an instant halt. It had been like this for days. He would
be working away, limber and comfortable, when out of the
blue something would ignite his slumbering senses. The
soft lilt of her voice as she petted her dog, a wet towel
tossed negligently over a laundry basket, the lingering tang
of her apricot shampoo.

Or her laughter, unexpected and unrestrained.

He ambled over to the open half-door, watched her
hands skate lightly over the horse's glossy coat. Yeah,
those hands doing pretty much anything that involved
stroking turned him on.

He cleared his throat. "This one's Star, right?"

She turned slowly, unsurprised, as if she had known he
was there. "Her full name is Stella Cadente."

"Shooting Star," he translated.

"You know Italian?"

"Enough. That name's a mouthful."

"It is." She smiled. "That's why we just call her Star.

Most of them have some Italian in their racing names and a shortened version for at-home use.''

''Monte?'' he asked.

''Is really Montefalco.''

''Gina?''

''Lollobrigida.'' A softly inquisitive expression lit her face. ''And I suppose you're really Nicholas.''

''Niccolo. The Italian version.''

Head slanted to one side, she considered it, considered him. And he knew he would do anything to hear that name, his full name, on her lips. *Please, Niccolo.*

''And what about you, Tamara?'' He drew the name out lushly, saw her hand still on the horse's flank for an instant before she resumed stroking. Felt his own body pulse. ''Why aren't you Tammy? Or Tara?''

''You have got to be kidding!''

He smiled at her melodramatic tone. ''Why do you call yourself T.C.?''

''Your guess is as good as mine.'' With an abrupt click, she attached the lead and brought the horse to the door. He didn't open it. He wasn't letting her out of this quite so easily.

''My guess is you decided your name was too girly. You thought someone named Tamara should wear pretty dresses and high heels and a perfume that smells like a rich garden party—''

''Enough, already,'' she interrupted, but a smile lurked around the corners of her mouth, and when that incredibly sexy mouth smiled it did more for him than any perfume or floaty dress.

Intent on teasing her embryonic smile to full life, he leaned over the half-door to sniff at her unperfumed throat...and the horse lunged, eyeballs rolling, mouth open.

Seven

In a knee-jerk reaction, he hauled her out the door and out of the path of a set of extremely large and not very white teeth.

"Hey, what was that all about?" She sounded breathless and slightly stunned.

"That beast masquerading as a horse would have taken a piece of your sweet little hide if I hadn't saved you."

"Oh, no, she was definitely gunning for *your* hide."

Her husky laughter rippled close to his throat, and when she shifted her weight, her hip rolled against his thigh. The fire on slow smolder in Nick's blood roared into full flame, but when his hands firmed on her back, she sobered instantly, pushing and twisting her way clear of his arms.

"She's never done that before," she murmured distractedly as the horse continued to stomp her hooves and toss her head.

"She's not the first female who's wanted to bite me."

"I bet she's the first to take an instant dislike to you."

"Ah, so *you* didn't."

A wry smile quirked her lips. "If you're fishing, Nick, forget it. I'm sure you've heard exactly how likable you are from plenty of people with far prettier words than me."

Yeah, but the thing was, he wanted to hear it from her. "If I was fishing, Tamara," he said slowly, clearly, seriously, "it wasn't for pretty words but honest ones."

Their gazes met and held, and Nick felt the heady rush of anticipation as keenly as if he stood strapped to his skis on a virgin Chugach ridge, about to go vertical. Then Star issued a shrill authoritative whinny that sliced right through the moment.

"That's her opinion," he said. "Now what about yours?"

"She's speaking for the both of us."

"If only I had a translator." He gestured toward Ug, who lay sleeping under the feeder. "Don't suppose she speaks horse?"

T.C. laughed. "Not so anyone would understand."

The mare stretched her long neck over the door in a gesture both elegant and eloquent, enticing Tamara to gather up the snaking lead *and* to scratch behind her ears.

Nick took a cautious step closer. Star rolled her eyes but kept her mouth closed. A promising start. Another measured step, a third, and she laid back her ears and kicked out at the wall. "Close enough, huh?"

The mare snorted.

"Seems I do speak some basic horse."

This time it was Tamara who snorted.

He rested a hand atop the door, waited. When the mare didn't take a piece out of it, he left it there, although he didn't take his eyes off her long black face.

"Can she run?" he asked.

"Like the wind."

"Is that how it feels, when you're driving? Like you're riding the wind?"

"Yes. That's it exactly."

He heard the smile in her voice, longed to see it on her lips, but when he started to turn, the mare bared her teeth. He kept his eyes firmly on those teeth.

"How did you know?" she asked.

"I'm guessing it's a bit like skiing. The wind, the rush, the sense of freedom. There are mountains like this beauty here, all mean and full of spirit, and then there are the rest."

She laughed softly. "Let me guess which you prefer."

He watched the big mare toss her head and swing her quarters around, left to right, as if impatient with the inactivity. "I'd like to try it," he said suddenly.

"You want to drive a horse?"

"I want to drive *this* horse. Will you teach me?"

"You're kidding! Was your first driving lesson in a Ferrari?"

Straight-faced, he looked down at her. "No. It was a Jaguar."

For a moment she simply stared back at him, eyes wide and incredulous; then she burst out laughing. The dulcet sound danced through his senses, filling him with a pleasure so pure it warmed him to the marrow of his bones.

"Well?" he asked when she finally recovered.

She glanced at the horse, who stood rolling her eyes at him. "When you can catch her, I'll teach you to drive her."

He took his time inspecting the horse, drawing out the suspense. Then he shrugged, pocketed his hands and stepped back. "Looks like I'll have to stick to the mountains."

"You're not going to try?"

He met the surprise in her eyes with a slow grin. "I know when I'm being had."

"Jase!" She sounded disgusted, but the look in her eyes approved his quick reading of the situation, and it warmed places Nick couldn't remember as anything but cold. "You could learn on another one. Monte's a real gentleman."

"Thanks," Nick said slowly. "But I seem to have developed a taste for the difficult, spirited type."

She met his unmistakable message head-on. And surprised him by not flinching. "Then it's a shame you have so little time. It could take months for a temperament like that to come around."

"Yeah?" His gaze skated from her face to the horse and back again. "Then it looks like we both lose out."

Despite his prior knowledge of Star's tricky temperament, T.C. had expected Nick to take up her challenge. She thought him arrogant enough to back himself in any difficult situation. Maybe he was, she thought consideringly, when she caught him standing at Star's stall door several days later.

Star took a tentative step forward and lowered her head to sniff at the hand resting on the door. Nick responded with a low laugh accompanied by some message of praise, and although distance muffled the words, T.C.'s body responded instantly to the mellow depth of his voice.

Exactly the same effect as he was having on Star, she realized. They had both started out kicking and snapping, and look at them now. Still wary, still inclined to take one step forward and two back, but both oh, so dangerously close to being seduced by a dark velvet voice and a steadily patient hand.

T.C. sighed with heavy resignation. Everything about the man—every damn thing!—was utterly alluring. His voice, the way he moved, that smile, the magic he made with a pot of pasta. Even his name was as exotically lush as the man himself. Niccolo Corelli. Why hadn't he turned out to be the conceited self-interested macho man she had imagined him to be? Why hadn't he been a carbon copy of Miles?

Heart in mouth, she watched Star toss her head and bare her teeth. Nick didn't move. He stood his ground, that one hand unmoving on the door, and she knew it was only a matter of time before the mare gave up the fight and came to him freely.

Did she stand any better chance of resisting?

She couldn't watch any longer, couldn't stand the apprehensive tension that churned in her stomach. Grabbing a head collar and lead, she strode to the door.

"I'm taking her out for some exercise," she said, more sharply than she had intended.

He didn't move, but she felt his steady scrutiny. "You want to take a passenger?"

What harm could it do? Maybe he would be as delighted by the experience as Joe had been on his first ride... although she doubted that. It seemed far too tame for a man who chased extreme adventure.

"Okay," she agreed eventually. "But this isn't a short cut to driving her. You're only the passenger."

"Yes, ma'am."

Ten minutes later, when she picked up the reins and swung herself into the jog-cart, she remembered why she had delayed this moment. Proximity. The bench seat was supposedly wide enough for three, but Nick took up an extraordinary amount of space.

So okay, she told herself, seated side by side there was bound to be contact, but that was no reason for her breath to hitch each time his sleeve brushed against hers. No reason for that bare whisper of sound to echo through her head, drowning out the cadent fall of hooves, the creak of springs, everything but the thunderous beat of her heart.

Annoyed by such a ridiculous state of hyperawareness, she clicked into a jog and edged to her right. A fat lot of good that did her. Nick simply spread to fit all available space, and now his thigh rested flush against hers. No big deal, she told herself, as she turned onto the track and settled Star into a steady relaxed pace. No bare flesh involved, a simple case of denim against denim.

All she needed was to redirect her senses.

Tipping her head back a fraction, she narrowed her field of perception, concentrating on the sun that touched her face, the strong wind that sifted through her hair and plastered her shirt against her skin. She absorbed the steady rocking rhythm of the horse's motion and felt herself start to relax.

"This is nice."

"Pardon?" She blinked, stared up at Nick.

"I said, I'm enjoying this." He nudged her with his elbow. "No need to look so surprised."

"I didn't think this would be quite your speed."

"You think I only like fast?"

Vivid images of all the things she had imagined him doing not-so-fast flashed through her mind. *Oh help, she did not need this now.* To hide the disconcerting wash of heat, she edged forward on the seat and pretended to reorganize the reins. She could feel his gaze on her, measuring, assessing.

"You love this, don't you?"

"Yes." She closed her eyes, felt the smile well up from somewhere deep within. "I love working with horses. I love how it makes me feel. It's hard to describe, but it's like…like this is where I belong."

"Did you feel that way about your father's home—where you were brought up?"

She thought about that. "I guess I did when I was younger. I know there were things I missed when I left, but there were other parts I couldn't wait to escape. But what I'm feeling here isn't about the physical things, it's about the spirit of the place and how it touches you. It's a sense of home." She laughed, more than a little self-conscious. "Do you know what I mean?"

When he didn't answer, she turned, caught the hint of a frown. "I can't say I've ever got that concept of home."

"What about Joe's Portsea house?"

"You've seen that place?" he asked with a mocking lift of one brow.

Not face-to-face, but she had seen pictures—it hardly fit the standard definition of home. But she wasn't talking about walls and lawns and manicured hedges, she was talking about feelings, and it seemed like he just didn't get it. She shrugged off an enormous wash of disappointment. Seems like she had been harboring a secret hope that he would fall in love with the spirit of Yarra Park as quickly and unconditionally as she had.

Only with Yarra Park, Tamara?

Do not go there, she told herself firmly. You'd do better to take this as a timely reminder of the footloose, uncluttered lifestyle he prefers...and of how little you have in common.

"You think I could do that?" he asked after a short, uncomfortable silence.

"I thought we agreed you were coming along as the passenger?"

He gave that lazy shrug he had down pat. "Worth a try."

T.C. snorted, then thought about it for another half-lap. "I'll let you drive if you agree to talk to a solicitor about me signing my half over to you."

"Don't you ever give up?"

"Worth a try," she countered with a mocking shrug.

His bark of laughter sounded like equal parts exasperation and admiration; then he surprised her with a casual, "Okay."

"Okay?"

"Yeah. I'll talk to my solicitor." He reached for the reins, but she didn't hand them over.

"When?"

FREE FREE
BOOKS! GIFT!

PLAY BANGO!

AND CLAIM 2 FREE BOOKS
AND A FREE GIFT!

BANGO

15	19	32	54	73
6	17	41	50	6
13	22	FREE	52	
5	24	44	46	
8	21	35	47	75

BANGO

9	19	44	52	71
4	20	32	50	68
11	18	FREE	53	63
7	27	36	60	72
3	28	41	47	64

BANGO

38	9	44	10	38
92	7	5	27	14
2	51	FREE	91	67
75	3	12	20	13
6	15	26	50	31

★ **No Cost!**
★ **No Obligation to Buy!**
★ **No Purchase Necessary!**

TURN THE PAGE TO PLAY →

PLAY BANGO!
AND GET THREE FREE GIFTS!

It looks like BINGO, it plays like BINGO but it's FREE!

HOW TO PLAY:

1. With a coin, scratch the Caller Card to reveal your 5 lucky numbers and see that they match your Bango Card. Then check the claim chart to discover what we have for you — 2 FREE BOOKS and a FREE GIFT — ALL YOURS, ALL FREE!

2. Send back the Bango card and you'll receive two brand-new Silhouette Desire® novels. These books have a cover price of $3.99 each in the U.S. and $4.50 each in Canada, but they are yours to keep absolutely free.

3. There's no catch. You're under no obligation to buy anything. We charge nothing — ZERO — for your first shipment. And you don't have to make any minimum number of purchases — not even one!

4. The fact is, thousands of readers enjoy receiving our books by mail from the Silhouette Reader Service™. They enjoy the convenience of home delivery…they like getting the best new novels at discount prices, BEFORE they're available in stores…and they love their *Heart to Heart* subscriber newsletter featuring author news, horoscopes, recipes, book reviews and much more!

5. We hope that after receiving your free books you'll want to remain a subscriber. But the choice is yours — to continue or cancel, any time at all! So why not take us up on our invitation, with no risk of any kind. You'll be glad you did!

YOURS FREE!
This exciting mystery gift is yours free when you play BANGO!

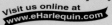
Visit us online at
www.eHarlequin.com

It's fun, and we're giving away

FREE GIFTS

to all players!

PLAY BANGO!

SCRATCH HERE! →

CALLER CARD

A7 B92 G27 O14 N5

YES!

Please send me the 2 free books and the gift for which I qualify! I understand that I am under no obligation to purchase any books as explained on the back of this card.

YOUR CARD ↘

BANGO

B	A	N	G	O
38	9	44	10	38
92	7	5	27	14
2	51	FREE	91	67
75	3	12	20	13
6	15	26	50	31

CLAIM CHART!

Match 5 numbers	2 FREE BOOKS & A MYSTERY GIFT
Match 4 numbers	2 FREE BOOKS
Match 3 numbers	1 FREE BOOK

326 SDL DHZ3

(S-D-OS-12/01)
225 SDL DHZ2

NAME   (PLEASE PRINT CLEARLY)

ADDRESS

APT.#   CITY

STATE/PROV.   ZIP/POSTAL CODE

The Silhouette Reader Service™ — Here's how it works:

Accepting your 2 free books and gift places you under no obligation to buy anything. You may keep the books and gift and return the shipping statement marked "cancel." If you do not cancel, about a month later we'll send you 6 additional novels and bill you just $3.34 each in the U.S., or $3.74 each in Canada, plus 25¢ shipping & handling per book and applicable taxes if any.* That's the complete price and — compared to cover prices of $3.99 each in the U.S. and $4.50 each in Canada — it's quite a bargain! You may cancel at any time, but if you choose to continue, every month we'll send you 6 more books, which you may either purchase at the discount price or return to us and cancel your subscription.

*Terms and prices subject to change without notice. Sales tax applicable in N.Y. Canadian residents will be charged applicable provincial taxes and GST.

If offer card is missing write to: Silhouette Reader Service, 3010 Walden Ave., P.O. Box 1867, Buffalo, NY 14240-1867

BUSINESS REPLY MAIL
FIRST-CLASS MAIL   PERMIT NO. 717-003   BUFFALO, NY

POSTAGE WILL BE PAID BY ADDRESSEE

SILHOUETTE READER SERVICE
3010 WALDEN AVE
PO BOX 1867
BUFFALO NY 14240-9952

NO POSTAGE
NECESSARY
IF MAILED
IN THE
UNITED STATES

''As soon as I can make an appointment.''

She shook her head. ''Not good enough. You're a Corelli—they'll make time for you.''

''Is tomorrow soon enough?''

''Morning?''

Laughing softly, he shook his head. ''Can I have breakfast first?''

Still, she hesitated.

''Come on. It's not so hard, is it, handing over the reins?''

Yes, Nick, she thought. It *is* hard and it's scary, putting yourself into someone else's hands. Relinquishing control.

With a deep sigh, she handed them over. He assumed the correct hold like a veteran. He didn't ask any of the usual learners' questions: *Is this okay? Am I doing this right?* With the natural arrogance of someone who did everything well, he simply knew he was doing fine.

''You have good hands,'' she praised reluctantly.

''So I've been told.''

By too many women, T.C. reminded herself. ''Do you pick up everything this easily?''

''Everything?''

''All those action-man things you do—the heli-skiing and rafting and climbing. Were they this easy?''

''If they were easy, there'd be no sense in doing them. No challenge.''

''What about the risk?''

He glanced across at her, his eyes as intensely blue as the autumn sky. Her heart flip-flopped. ''It doesn't hurt to take a few risks, Tamara, to push outside your comfort zone. That's what makes you feel alive.''

''No. *This* is what makes me feel alive.''

Something in his expression as he took in her resolutely spoken words did strange things to her heart. She felt the compelling draw of his gaze but refused to meet it. The

need to run, to escape, rode her hard, and she blew out a
frustrated breath. ''You want to try another gear?''

''Yeah. I feel like I could blow off some steam.''

''Then I'd better take over.''

As she took the reins, his fingers grazed across hers.
Awareness charged through her system, causing her to
fumble. Star reacted by grabbing the bit and plunging forward. For a while T.C. needed all her skill to restrain the
horse's enthusiastic charge, but gradually the mare responded to her coaxing hands and soothing words.

As she came back into hand, T.C. realized Nick was
laughing—not with reactionary hysteria, but with sheer unrestrained pleasure. His mood tapped straight into T.C.'s
adrenaline overload. Unable to restrain herself, she let go
her own wild tension-relieving whoop. The sound caught
and lifted in the breeze, mingling with the thick red dust
that rose in their wake.

Star picked up on the mood in a trice. T.C. felt her
suppressed power shudder through the reins and let her
run. They sped a full circuit on the very edge of control,
and it was only as they eased back to a more sedate pace
that she realized Nick had needed to grab hold of something during that helter-skelter spurt.

That something happened to be her leg.

She didn't need to look down to picture his palm span-
ning the width of her thigh, his long splayed fingers boldly
defined by the near-white of her faded jeans. Desire, as
wild and unruly as that mad dash, bit with vicious teeth.
The only thing holding her in check was the sound practical fact that the reins in her hands prevented her reaching
out and putting them on him.

Gradually Star came back to a jog, then a long, loping
walk, and the air around them thickened with the sound
of her elevated breathing, the sharp smell of exertion.

''That was...unexpected.'' Slowly, deliberately, he slid

his hand from her leg. "Kind of makes me wonder what else you're capable of when you let go."

His meaning should have sent her scuttling for cover, but it seemed like that high-speed ride had blown away more than steam and tension. It must have blown away a large dose of common sense, for she smiled as she said, "I guess it's lucky I've got these reins in my hands."

"Lucky for who?"

Lucky for me, T.C. responded silently as she turned Star back toward the stables and sanity.

Jason was waiting at the stables, full of questions. Had Nick really taken the reins? How fast did they go? Was it a rush? The necessary explanations—together with the mundane task of unharnessing—went a long way toward settling the smoldering tension.

They were both laughing easily at something Jason said when they reached for the girth strap at the same time. Their hands touched. The jolt—electric sharp, lightning fast—zinged through her, and she was instantly completely aware of him. The grave stillness of his gaze, his earthy male scent, the sheen of heat on his skin, the pulsing beat of his heart. If she closed her eyes, she swore she would hear the blood surging through his veins. But she didn't close her eyes. They had fixed on the sensual curve of his mouth, so near she could feel his breath on her face.

Oh help. If he kisses me, I'm sunk.

His fingers curled around hers. His thumb stroked once across the back of her hand, and her insides turned to liquid.

Oh help. If he doesn't kiss me, I'll die.

"Are you two going to undo that buckle or stand about holding hands all afternoon?" Jase asked with a disgusted snort.

T.C. reclaimed her hand and avoided meeting anyone's eyes. Jason gathered up the remaining gear and took it off to the tack room. Nick cleared his throat and asked if he should hose Star down. Star snorted and pawed at the ground, and Ug trotted in from an afternoon's rat hunting.

Everything back to normal, T.C. thought, although her pulse still skittered all over the yard like an unbroken colt. She watched Nick lead Star away and thought about the chores still to be done. She would rather watch Nick, or talk to Nick, or go take a long shower, then stretch out on her bed to think about Nick.

Everything definitely far from normal, she thought uneasily. What was wrong with her? She still hadn't moved several minutes later when a spray of water arced high above the concrete wall enclosing the wash-bay, closely followed by a muffled oath. By the time she arrived Nick looked about as wet as the horse with the hose clasped between its teeth.

At the sound of her strangled laughter, his head whipped around. "Are you here to help or for the entertainment?"

She folded her arms across her chest. "Oh, definitely for the show."

"Which is undoubtedly funnier from where you're standing."

At precisely that moment Star turned her head, gave him an innocent look and dropped the hose.

"Thanks for your cooperation," he muttered as the hose, still spurting water, snaked out of his reach. "Would you get that for me?"

She shouldn't have taken that call for assistance at face value. She should have noticed the narrowing of his gaze, the unholy light in his eyes. But she was too busy chortling at his predicament.

She gathered the hose and brought it to him at the front of the bay, and Nick casually stepped around her to block the exit. Snookered. Her eyes widened on the weapon she had unwittingly handed him. "Oh, no," she breathed, backing up the four steps it took to hit the wall. "You wouldn't."

"No?" he asked, and his grin felt more than smug. It felt positively feral. "Are you sure about that?"

No, she wasn't. He caught the furtive glances as she assessed her chances of making it to the tap before him.

"You can try, but you'll end up very wet."

"I have a feeling I'm going to get wet either way."

"You deserve to."

"If you'd been in my shoes, you'd have seen the funny side." A small bubble of merriment escaped her lips as she tipped her head back against the wall. Then she caught his unamused expression and lifted her hands in the traditional gesture of surrender. "Okay, I can take a little water. Do your worst."

Hell. She was standing there with her shirt pulled deliciously tight across her breasts, her green eyes glimmering a wicked challenge, daring him to do his worst? His *best* right this minute would involve nailing her to that wall with his body and his mouth and sucking the remnants of laughter from her full bottom lip. His *worst* would involve nailing her to the wall, full stop.

"Maybe you won't get wet if you ask nicely."

"You want me to say please?"

"I want you to say *please, Nick.*"

She moistened her lips. His body responded with extravagant haste—to the glimpse of her tongue, to her softly parted lips, to the anticipatory pleasure of hearing those two little words, her voice breathless and husky.

Please, Niccolo.

She struck with lightning speed, catching him at a distracted disadvantage...but not for long. With his superior reach and strength, it was never going to be a fair fight, although her tenacity ensured that they both ended up very wet.

Very wet and very close.

When Nick finally restrained her, he was achingly aware of how close. The second their eyes met, she stopped struggling. With her body wedged flush against his, he could feel her tightly coiled tension, could see both the heat of sensual knowledge and a familiar wariness in her wide green eyes, and wondered how long before she started running. He thought about begging.

Please, Tamara.

His fingertips trailed across her abdomen, stilled when they found the small gap where her shirt had pulled clear of her jeans. He rested his palm where cold wet cotton met warm satin skin, heard her sharply drawn breath and waited for her to snap at him, to pull away, to slap his hand.

She didn't move.

He looked down at the wet shirt plastered to the soft mounds of her breasts, at the clearly visible outline of her erect nipples, and his stomach clenched tight in an instant surge of need. He dipped his mouth and nipped at the earlobe that peeped through her softly mussed hair, at the smooth curve of her neck, at the point where that neck met her shoulder. He tasted the surface chill of cold water, then the fresh warmth of her skin, and, deeper still, the heat of pure desire.

He wondered if it was possible to drown in lust.

Everything about her aroused him, but nothing so much as the soft yielding in her eyes as her body swayed into his, as she cupped his face between her hands and muttered, "Will you please just kiss me."

"Please, Nick," he prompted, as his hands swept over her back. He bit her bottom lip, dragged it between his teeth, then slowly released it. A low frustrated moan built in her throat and resounded through his blood, stirring him, inflaming him...but it wasn't the words he needed to hear. "Say it," he demanded.

Eyes glittering, she moistened her lips, but they remained silent. Desperate hands slid into his hair, then held him steady as she stretched on her toes and planted her lips against his. She kissed him with openmouthed carnality, encouraging his tongue into the warm, moist cavern of her mouth with a boldness that sizzled to his groin. He gripped her more tightly, his hands curving over her behind, drawing her nearer, molding the softness of her belly to the pulsing heat of his arousal.

A groan rumbled deep in his chest as her hands stroked from his shoulders to his waist. He swore he heard steam sizzle in their wake. He did hear a low hiss whistle through his teeth as those hands continued their downward path, stroking over his butt, making him ache to be naked, skin to skin. Inside and out.

He walked her backward. Two steps and she was against the wall. Hands planted either side of her face, he bent his knees to bring himself down to her height, so he could look right into her sultry green eyes while he rocked his hips against her. Just once. Then he closed his eyes and struggled to control the primal need that pumped savagely through him.

Man, had he ever been so hard? So desperate?

She touched his face, her fingers a cool, gentle contrast to the furnace in his blood. "Please, Nick," she whispered as they locked gazes.

Finally.

"Please what?" he growled. "Tell me what you want, Tamara."

A shadow crossed her face. Indecision. She blinked it away, bit her lip.

Hell. Nick blew out a short, frustrated breath. His splayed fingers closed, curled into tight fists. "Right this minute I'm about as close to exploding as I've ever been with my clothes on. But nothing more is going to happen until you look me in the face and tell me what you want. Just so there's no mistaking. Your choice of words."

A slow flush bled into her face. "I can't say...that."

Imagined alternatives to *that* drove a thick groan from Nick. Weak with wanting, he rested his forehead against hers. He thought about prompting her, tempting her with more kisses. Rejected it. She needed to make this decision all on her own. In the morning, he wanted to turn his head on the pillow, open his eyes and look right into sea-green eyes softly glazed with desire, not clouded with regret.

He took stock of his surroundings for the first time in fifteen minutes. "I guess we're lucky Jase didn't walk around the corner. Or that one of your smarter animals didn't decide to break this up."

Her half-laugh, half-sigh flowed warm against his throat. "Thank you."

"For?"

"Not pressing me. Giving me a chance to get sane about this."

"Ah, that would be my noble streak."

He eased back far enough to look down into her face. The undertow of insecurity lurking in the depths of those amazingly expressive eyes grabbed him hard. For a moment he felt winded, as raw desire made space for a strong surge of tenderness. He brushed the backs of his fingers along her cheekbone, pressed a kiss to her nose, another to her lips, a third to her chin, then pushed himself away from the wall. Away from temptation.

"I think this would be a good time to go ring my solicitor friend, see if he can't fit a Corelli in this afternoon." He touched a finger to her lips, then stepped away. "Don't go getting too sane about this, okay?"

Slumped against the wall, T.C. watched him walk away. She wanted to call him back while she could still taste him on her lips and feel him on her skin, while the fever of need still burned in her blood. Before the return of sanity. But what would she say?

Yes, I want you to make love to me. I want your scorching kisses and velvet-cloaked caresses, your incendiary words and soft midnight whispers. I want to feel beautiful and strong and craved; I want to feel like a woman who is your equal. But how could she call him back when her insecurities cast such a thick shroud over her desire?

She feared the afterward, when his male hunger was slaked, when he tossed her a casual goodbye and a consolatory kiss, then sauntered off into the sunset. She feared the desperate ache of withdrawal from the loving she'd grown addicted to, and most of all she feared the loneliness of the nights that stretched ahead with only her hollow pride for company.

It was those fears that constricted her throat and dried her mouth as she watched him walk away. It would take less than a night of loving to become addicted to Nick, and despite the power of the attraction, despite everything he could make her feel, he was still a man who didn't know the meaning of home, a man who liked to move on. He was still perfectly unsuitable for her.

Eight

When he drove down the road less than an hour later, she should have been relieved, able to breathe again, but instead she thought about the day when he would head down that same road en route for the airport, and it felt as if her heart plummeted to her toes. And maybe it stayed there, because her feet seemed to drag heavily through every long drawn-out hour of the day, right up until the setting sun painted the horizon in multicolored dusk.

Then a sense of expectancy quickened her blood, and any noise prompted her heart to bound into her throat. She tried to distract herself with television, flicking indifferently past a score of channels, thinking that at least the volume would prevent her ears from straining for the sound of his vehicle. Fat chance. Minute by minute, her restlessness grew until she couldn't sit still any longer.

She punched the off button on a noisy sitcom and blew out an exasperated puff of air. How lame was she? Sitting here in the semidarkness waiting for him to come home, not even knowing if he would drive back tonight. And if he did, what would she say to him? Certainly nothing that he wanted to hear.

Tell me what you want, Tamara.

Well, Nick, I want what you want, with the same intense hunger I felt in your kisses, in that one grinding pulse of your hips, in your voice, so hot and tight. But I want it every day for the rest of my life.

No, she didn't think he would want to hear anything quite that honest.

That's it, she declared with savage purpose. I will not sit here torturing myself any longer. I need company. She tried Cheryl's number, but no one answered. Undeterred, she changed into narrow white jeans and her favorite lime-green stretch shirt, brushed her hair until it gleamed with life, touched her lips with gloss and headed out the door.

At the sound of an approaching vehicle, her hand stilled on the lock. Not his car, she realized after her pulse had done its first crazy stop-and-go, but the low throaty roar of a powerful bike. The sound resonated through her body and she didn't move—*couldn't move*—as a single headlight arced across the garden, then caught her in its searching eye. Seconds later the bike throbbed to a halt beside her.

It was a big, dark, dangerous beast of a bike, the kind that made her blood pump faster with reckless images of the forbidden. The kind that fit Nick as perfectly as his black biker's jacket and faded denim jeans.

He killed the engine, and the silence vibrated around her, keeping time with the accelerated beat of her heart. The sight of his booted feet, spread wide and planted on either side of the monster bike, made her own legs tremble. Her gaze floated upward, all the way to his full-face helmet, and even through the smokily opaque visor she could feel the intensity of his gaze.

Watching her.

She moistened arid lips, felt his gaze touch her, burn

her, as he removed his helmet. The contrast from smoky shades of darkness to pure light-filled blue was breathtaking. It was like looking into the center of the sun. Then he lifted a hand to rake the unruly hair back from his face, breaking the searing connection.

T.C. cleared her throat. "Where did you find this baby?"

Humor sparked in his molten eyes. "The stork sure didn't bring it."

"It would have had to be a mighty big stork," she mused, moving around the bike, compelled to look, to touch.

"You like her?"

"No way is this a feminine machine."

"No? She reminds me of Stella. All that brute power, scarcely contained."

She smiled. Yes, she could see that. Liked that he'd drawn the comparison, and the way he called Star the Italian version of her name. The less ordinary, the more exotic.

"Plus I don't much care for the notion of throwing my leg over anything I refer to as 'he.'"

Well, no. She could see that, too. She touched a fingertip to the handlebar, cleared the heat from her throat. "You asked if I like her…. I'm not sure anyone could simply *like* a beauty like this."

"You're right. I'd forgotten how it feels to ride one of these. To open her up and feel all that power surge through you."

He laughed, the sound low and throaty and as shockingly arousing as his words. T.C. rubbed her hands over her goose-bumpy arms. She felt his gaze follow the action, caressing her bare skin into complete awareness, brushing the length of her throat, resting on the curve of her waist. Touching the painfully tight thrust of her nipples.

"You're going out?" All the laughter was gone from his voice.

"Yes." *But if you ask me to stay, if you ask me to take a ride with you…*

He didn't ask, and in the awkward silence she found herself circling the bike again.

"So…did she follow you home or what?" She trailed her fingers across the back of the wide leather seat. It was sleek and surprisingly cool, a stark contrast to the rough heated edges of her own mood.

"Graeme loaned her to me for a couple of days."

"Graeme?"

"A partner in Kermit's firm. We were at school together."

"Your solicitor friend," she guessed. Then, "I can't imagine a suit riding one of these."

He shook his head. "There you go with your preconceptions again."

She leaned back against the door of her truck and folded her arms across her chest. "What do you mean by 'again'?"

"You'd made up your mind about me long before we met." He climbed off the bike, his expression unreadable. "That's why you've been so wary of me from day one. Because of who you think I am."

What could she say? That she'd been building a defense? That she feared she would fall for him totally, completely, inextricably? All she could say was, "I have to go."

He uttered a polite, "Have a nice time," turned and walked away.

T.C. was halfway to town before she realized she hadn't asked him what he'd found out from his solicitor friend.

Nick hadn't hesitated when Graeme offered to loan him the Ducati. He'd thought the ride home would help cool his simmering blood, but the moment he'd seen her standing there with her tight jeans and gloss-slicked mouth, he'd felt the burn like a flamethrower in his gut.

It had burned harder when she'd refused to talk to him—when she'd run away again—and hadn't let up the whole night, not even when he heard her vehicle cross the stockgrid into the yard. Not yet eleven, he noted. She can't have been having much fun. He tried to smile but barely managed a sneer.

Her soft footfalls sounded in the hallway. He heard them pause outside the office door; then he heard nothing but the wild pounding of his heart. His nostrils flared instinctively, and he swore he could smell her light enticing scent. He knew her essence filled his senses, had done so all week, ever since that first kiss.

He was instantly hard, intensely hard.

If you knock on that door, there'll be no more noble streak. There'll only be me and you and enough fire to incinerate this whole county.

He felt the sheen of heat on his skin and the coiled tension of every muscle as he sat, barely breathing, poised like some big cat intent on its prey. When he heard her footsteps retreat toward her room he almost howled with frustration. Instead he cursed whatever odd quirk of conscience or honor or pure male pride insisted he wait for her to come to him.

T.C. rose early and pushed herself hard throughout the next day, hoping to drive yesterday from her mind. "Might as well hope you'll grow wings and morph into Pegasus," she told Duke as she rugged him late in the afternoon.

The phone was ringing as she came into the house, tired from physical exertion and edgy with the prospect of facing Nick. She grabbed the receiver without thinking. "Hello?"

Her greeting was met with a beat of silence long enough

for her heart to bound and lodge in her throat. Surely not…not after a week of silence.

"Hello?"

T.C. pressed a hand to her chest and closed her eyes. Thank God! There was someone there. A voice. A woman.

"Hello?" the woman repeated. "Is anyone there?"

"Yes. Sorry. This is Tamara Cole. Can I help you?"

Another curious beat of silence. "Now I'm confused. I was sure George said you'd moved."

"Who is this?"

"Oh, how rude of me." The woman sounded more richly amused than contrite. "I'm Sophie Corelli. Could I possibly speak to Nicky?"

Nicky?

"I've been trying to reach him for days, and he never returns my calls."

"I'll see if I can find him," T.C. said weakly, although if he was in the office, he would have picked up Sophie's call. God forbid she would have to hunt him down in his bedroom or shower.

Cordless handset clutched to her chest, she peered around the partly open office door. No one home. Mind made up to take a message, she went in but found her purpose immediately overtaken by curiosity. Carefully she set down the phone and looked around. There wasn't much to see.

A blank computer screen, paperwork stacked in several untidy piles, a couple of notes scrawled even less legibly than his shopping list, a tray of computer printouts—charts of some kind—and sitting on top of them a pair of metal-rimmed glasses. She ran a tentative finger along one earpiece and told herself the strange little tug around her heart was the reassuring notion of Nick with an imperfection, not the incredibly endearing image of him wearing glasses.

"Looking for something?"

She turned quickly, backing away from the desk as if

she'd been caught snooping...which of course she hadn't.
Luckily the bookcase provided support for her sudden
weak-kneed breathlessness when he came into the room,
wet hair flopping over his forehead, shirt untucked and
hanging open.

All endearing thoughts evaporated in an instant haze of
heat.

"Tamara?"

"Oh...a...um...call. For you." Four words, four syllables, yet she had trouble stringing them together. Swal-
lowing, she looked away, focused on the phone instead.
"It's your sister."

"That narrows the field to four. Any idea which one?"

"Oh. Yes. It's Sophie."

The corner of his mouth twitched—with irritation?—as
he swung into the chair and swiveled it toward the desk.
When he reached for the phone his chambray shirt
stretched taut across the breadth of his shoulders, and her
attention was drawn to several tendrils of hair curling over
his collar.

*Oh, help! This room is definitely too small and too
poorly ventilated.*

"Sophie? You still there?"

He propped the phone between his chin and shoulder
while he buttoned his shirt. What was it with him and
dressing in her presence? She edged along the wall until
she heard his weight shift in the chair and felt the dark
unsettling touch of his gaze. Ignore it, she told herself. But
when she started to move, more overtly this time, he simply rolled his chair into her path.

Satisfied she wasn't going anywhere but incredibly irritated by her attempt, Nick turned his attention to the
phone call. "How did you get this number?" he asked at
the end of Sophie's introductory small talk. Sophie held a
masters in small talk.

"From your partner, natch."

Nick swore. Sophie laughed. Tamara looked up from contemplating her toes, then away again just as quickly.

"George said you were only in the country for a day or two. Math was never my strong suit, but I can add. You've been there well over a week now. What gives, Nicky?"

"Ever heard of taking a break?"

"Didn't you just get back from a break—in Alaska, of all places?"

"Your point?"

"Hmm...wrong season for skiing, and I don't recall any decent climbs or white water nearby, so it must be a woman. Oh my God, is that why Joe's little woman is still there? You are too much, Nicky!"

"She wasn't Joe's—" He stopped himself right there. Swore silently when Sophie crowed with malicious delight. Willed Tamara to look at him, but she continued to stare fixedly at her toes.

"This is *soooo* priceless," Sophie cooed. "I can't wait to share."

"It's none of George's business."

"You think he hasn't made it his business? He's been in a hellish snit about your little bequest, and he can't bear to have you in the same country. What I can't decide is why he's still paranoid. Is it still about Emily?"

Nick scrubbed a hand over his face. "Don't call him to make trouble, Soph. Tell him I don't want anything of his, especially his wife, and I'll be out of the country this time next week. Will you do that?"

"Why not?" He could hear her shrug. "No skin off my nose."

After he recradled the receiver, Nick realized he had been gripping it with viselike intensity. Straightening his fingers was actually painful. Man, but he hated the way Sophie's troublemaking could still steam him...almost as much as George's paranoia. Was it any wonder he chose to live on the opposite side of the world? With barely contained frustration, he shoved his chair away from the desk and found Tamara eyeing the door.

"Thinking of running away again?"

Her fitful gaze jerked back to his. "It's not quite like that."

"Isn't it?" He slapped a hand down on the arm of his chair. "You'd have been locked behind your bedroom door ten minutes ago if I hadn't blocked your exit."

"I'm sorry. It's just…"

"Just what? Just that you don't have the guts to talk straight to me?"

She recoiled sharply, as if the words had stung, and Nick wanted nothing more than to back down, to apologize to her, and that only made him angrier.

"Stay, for once," he bit out. "Talk to me."

"I don't know how to talk to a man like you."

"A man like me?"

With a rough curse, he thrust his chair forward, startling her into knocking several books from the shelf at her back. Nick ignored their heavy tumble to the floor. He felt an insane urge to keep going, to surge out of the chair and demonstrate what sort of edgy, frustrated man he had become.

"Tell me, Tamara. What kind of man do you think I am?" he asked with dangerous calm.

"The kind I can't relate to. Joe drove me nuts with his stories. Nick's gone kayaking in Peru. Nick's joining an Everest expedition. To me your life is… I don't know…larger than life."

"What about this past week, Tamara? Don't you feel like you've been relating to me, cuz it sure as hell felt like we were relating down in that shower bay yesterday."

Hot color flared in her cheeks, hot memories in her gaze; then she looked away, and Nick cursed out loud. He hadn't meant to bring that up. *What was it with her?* She had a way of getting under his skin so damn quick he barely felt the pinprick, and right this minute she was so far under he could feel his skin stretched taut.

"Don't you think it's time you started judging me with your own eyes instead of on an old man's ramblings?"

That brought her gaze charging back to his, so heated it seared him with green fire. "How can you talk about Joe like that? He wasn't some rambling old man, he was your father!"

"He wasn't my father."

She stared at him, stunned into silence.

Gaze fixed on the ceiling, he rocked back in his chair and expelled a short harsh breath. "I don't know why I said that. It's not something I talk about." Not because he was ashamed, but because it didn't make any difference to who he was. Not anymore.

"Maybe you should." T.C. watched his lips set in a firm line as he rocked back to face her. Their gazes locked and held for five long seconds, and the guarded vulnerability in his expression squeezed her heart. She stood with the breath backing up in her lungs while her eyes willed him to explain. These next few minutes held the key to understanding Nick—not the Nick of her preconceptions but the real Nick—and that key would likely open the door on a whole new set of feelings. Strangely, the thought didn't scare her as much as it should have.

"You sure you want to hear this?" he asked.

"I *need* to hear it."

He scrubbed a hand across his face. "Where to start."

"The beginning's usually a good place."

"Not in my case." His smile was grim, humorless. "I don't even know much about my beginning. My mother was a hooker and an addict, or an addict and a hooker. Whatever. My father could have been anyone."

His gaze held hers, and the expression in the depths of his eyes was as harsh as his words, daring her to flinch or to look away. She did neither—she simply prompted him to continue. "What happened to your mother?"

"She was a distant cousin of Joe's, but they'd never met. They shared the same surname and that's about it. Apparently she saw his picture on the cover of a magazine, did some research on their family connection and decided to try blackmail. Joe didn't bite. A couple weeks later she OD'd. Joe's number was in her things, and the authorities thought he might be next of kin."

"So he took you in."

"What else could he do?" He shrugged, the gesture tense and self-conscious, and so unlike Nick. Her stomach twisted painfully.

"He could have done nothing." Except they both knew that wouldn't have been an option for Joe. "How old were you?"

"Eight."

She pictured a small bewildered child, wrenched from the familiar into a stranger's world, and she wondered if that was the reason he didn't get the concept of home. "That can't have been easy," she said slowly.

"It was easy enough on me. I got to eat regular meals and sleep in the same bed every night." His harsh exhalation didn't much resemble a laugh. "It was tough on Joe's wife, though. She already had five kids."

"I imagine she had plenty of help."

His gaze was sharp, almost hard. "Yeah, she had a housekeeper and a cook, but I wasn't talking about that."

No. She could see that. He was talking about the emotional side, the impact of a new kid thrown into that headstrong, spoiled, Corelli brood. It would have been tough on all of them, but especially so on Nick. She felt that as a dull ache in her heart.

"Joe talked so much about you, yet he never mentioned this. Never hinted, not even in the letter. As far as he was concerned, you are his son—that's why he talked about you so much. He was proud of you. He missed you. He *loved* you. He *was* your father, Nick.''

''Yeah, well, like you, I wished he was.''

He leaned back in his chair, his posture a negligent contrast to the tense lines of his face and the shadows that darkened his eyes. For a second she battled the urge to close the space between them, to wrap her arms around him and soothe away those shadows...but only for a second. Then she lost the battle. She went down on her knees, placed a gentle hand on his knee.

''He loved you as his son, Nick.''

A muscle twitched in his cheek. His gaze glittered with hard cynicism as it shifted from her face to her hand, then back again. ''What's this, Tamara? You can't put your hand on me in honest desire but you can out of pity?''

She shook her head, but he was already getting to his feet, stepping around her.

''I don't want your pity. That's not why I told you.'' He stopped at the door, blew out a harsh breath. ''I don't know why I told you.''

''It's not about pity, Nick. It's about understanding.''

''You think because I told you about my background you suddenly understand me?'' His voice was as hard as his eyes, as uncompromising as his stance. ''I'm the same man I was this afternoon. Nothing's changed.''

But as he walked away, she told herself he was wrong.

He was still the same man, but everything else had changed now that she knew the boy he had been. Now she saw reasons for a man to search for his place in the world, to prove himself better than his background, to earn everything he owned on his own merits and not from the benevolence of his adoptive family.

She only hoped that knowledge would give her the courage to go to him and put her hand on him in honest desire.

Nine

Sixteen hours later Nick watched a dark blue BMW glide to a halt outside the stables. He knew who would own such a vehicle even before the driver stepped out, smoothed an imaginary wrinkle from his jacket, then did an exaggerated backstep away from Ug's welcome.

On some other day Nick might have found that comical, but right now he wasn't in the mood for funny. He wasn't in the mood for visitors, either, especially unwelcome ones, although after Sophie's phone call, her brother's appearance wasn't exactly unexpected.

He pushed his wheelbarrow into the next stall and pitched a fork into the straw bedding. When the hair on the back of his neck stood to attention, he knew he had company.

"Lost, bro?" he asked without looking up.

"I heard you found yourself some dirt to play around in, but I thought Sophie was referring to something else."

Nick tightened his grip on the pitchfork. Told himself

the reality of wrapping it around George's puny neck wouldn't be nearly as satisfying as the imagining. He dug deep under a pile of soiled straw, lifted and tossed it in one deft motion, then raised innocent brows when it overshot the barrow to land square on a pair of highly polished Italian loafers.

"Sorry about that."

And in the silence that followed he realized he *was* sorry—not for sullying George's shoe leather but for succumbing to the moment. It was a puerile response, and it hadn't made him feel a whole lot better. Some, but not nearly enough.

George's thin lips pursed in distaste. "Could we continue our discussion in the office?"

"What, exactly, are we discussing?"

"I know of a party who's keen to buy into the horse business. He liked the sound of this place."

"You remember our meeting, the day I arrived? Which part of 'I don't want your help' didn't you understand?"

A quick flush stained George's skin. "I was approached by an associate of Joe's who assumed I was the new owner. I saw a chance to help you out."

"Well, thanks for driving all the way out here to help me out, bro, but I'm not looking for a buyer."

"What do you mean?" George's flush deepened to a dull red. "You live overseas. What would you want with a place here?"

None of your damned business. That was Nick's instant response, the one he would have given a week ago. Back then he would have grinned to show he couldn't care less, before he turned his back and sauntered away. But it seemed like his attitude had changed, probably because he had grown sick and tired of Tamara walking away instead of talking about whatever was bothering her. For the first time in fourteen years, he decided it was worth talking to George.

"Whether or not Sophie gave you my message, it bears repeating. I don't want anything that belongs to you, and that includes what you refer to as your help.

"Yes, I do live overseas—I made that choice because it was easier on everyone and it suited me fine. I wanted to make my own life. I proved what I could do without Joe's help and despite my background."

Flushed and tight-lipped, George opened his mouth to interrupt, but Nick held up a hand.

"I'm almost done. Hear me out, okay? My decision to keep Yarra Park has nothing to do with you. None of my life has anything to do with you. Not anymore."

"That's not much of an attitude toward family."

"You want to talk about attitude to family?" Nick's voice was as steel-sharp as the prongs on the pitchfork in his hand. "What about your efforts to contact me when Joe took ill? What about that solicitor's letter after he died? He might not have been my blood father, but he brought me up as his son and as your brother. Don't you think I deserved better?"

"You didn't deserve anything—" George said spitefully as he inclined his head toward the manure-filled barrow. "Except where you are right now. What you're doing here is a fitting job for you."

"I suggest you get the hell out of here before I do something fitting with this pitchfork."

"We both know you won't risk that," George sneered, but he edged out of Nick's reach. "This time Joe isn't here to stick up for you. This time I *would* press charges."

"He never took sides. He did what was fair."

"He might have tried, but we all know you were his favorite. That's why he left you this place."

"You got the Portsea house and the chairmanship and your share of the rest of it. Why are you so stuck on this one small thing?"

"Because it's not a small thing—it's the thing that mattered most!'' The words erupted from George's tight lips, as if the lid had been lifted on a pressure cooker of festering resentment.

''And you think that if I sell, it will make a difference to the way you feel? Hell, George, if I sent you Yarra Park in gift wrapping it wouldn't make a lick of difference. You don't know why Joe did it this way, and you can't change the fact that he did. It simply is.''

He met the bitterness in George's eyes, a bitterness he knew was burning the other man up from the inside out.

''Don't you think it's time you got over this jealousy thing? You're thirty-four years old. You have a wife and a family, the home and the job you wanted. Isn't it time you concentrated your energy on what you have instead of what you can't have?''

George had no comeback. First time in his life, Nick thought, as he watched him turn on his heel and stalk away. He wasn't sure if his message got through, wasn't sure if it ever would, but at least he had tried.

He would have returned to his chore, except a sense of foreboding niggled at his gut. He put the tool aside and walked out to the front of the stables as the sleek dark sedan pulled to a stop halfway down the driveway.

Hell. Tamara and Jason were on their way back from the track, but only one horse stopped as George climbed out of his car. Nick's shoulder muscles bunched and his hands curled into fists as he watched the short exchange, knowing that whatever George had to say wouldn't be pleasant. It also didn't take long. The car took off in a furious spurt of dust, while Tamara headed her horse to the barn at a sedate walk.

She swung out of the cart, seemingly unperturbed, but then she fumbled with the simple clasp on her helmet, cursed, and Nick noticed the tremor in her normally sure hands. He placed his on her shoulders, stilling her with gentle insistence.

"What did he say to you?"

"Nothing that bears repeating."

"That bad, huh?" He slid his hands down her arms, back up again. "He left here looking for a whipping boy— you just happened to be convenient. Don't take it personally."

"He said you threatened him with a pitchfork. If I'd had one handy, I'd have done more than threaten." Her eyes glittered with temper, and Nick felt relief radiate through his whole being. She wasn't shaking with fear; she was shaking with rage.

"Yeah, well, as tempting as that sounds, it would have done more harm than good."

T.C. snorted.

"I did hit him once, a long while ago. If Joe hadn't interceded, he'd have charged me with assault."

"I hope you hit him hard."

"Flattened his nose, but it wasn't nearly as satisfying as I'd thought it would be." He rubbed his hands over her shoulders and down her arms again, smoothing her brittle temper as quickly as it had flared. "Plus it gave him something else to hate me for."

Joe had told her his sons didn't get along, but he had never told her why—whether something specific had caused a rift or if they simply clashed on everything. Hate was a strong word, but that was exactly what she had seen burning in George's eyes when he stopped to hurl insults at her.

He took his hands from her arms, and T.C. immediately felt the loss of calm. She felt edgy and restive, as if *she* needed to run a few laps of the track. Returning to work wasn't an option. She turned and called out to Jason, "Will you finish up here?" before swinging back to Nick. "You want to take a walk?"

"Are we going to get wet?" he asked, inclining his head toward the clouds gathering on the southern horizon.

"Not for hours yet." She started walking and felt him beside her, matching his stride to hers. "Is getting Yarra Park one of the things George hates you for?" she wondered out loud.

"One of a long list. There's a whole heap of paranoia going on in his head that I can't begin to understand. He hated the attention I got when I first came to live with them, and I don't think he ever got over it. The older we got, the worse his jealousy got."

"What was he jealous of?"

"School reports, who made the football team, praise from Joe. Anything and everything."

"You know, I can almost see his point of view."

"Yeah?"

Feeling the curiosity in his gaze, she tilted her face to meet it. "Yeah. I have this picture forming of you two as teenagers. Nick, a couple of years younger but already bigger, stronger, better looking. I bet you made all the teams, got better grades, and every time George brought a girl home, she took one look at you and forgot big brother."

She smiled, wanting to ease the moment, but Nick didn't respond. And his words to Sophie came vividly to mind. *I don't want anything of his, especially his wife.* Holy toledo. She moistened her dry mouth.

"This fight you had when you flattened his nose...was it over a girl?"

"Yes and no." He paused long enough that she thought he wouldn't continue. Their initial get-me-out-of-here strides had slowed to a bare stroll, and the mood felt as ominous as the gathering storm clouds.

"Emily had been going out with George for a while when she told him she had this thing for me. I don't know if she really did, or if she just had some kind of agenda. I mean, I hardly even knew her—I'd met her a couple of times around the pool, but mostly I steered clear of George's friends. Whatever it was..." He lifted one shoulder in a stiff gesture of dismissal. ''…it brought on the fight that had been brewing for years.''

''Is that why you went away?''

''I would have gone anyway.''

They stopped at the boundary fence. T.C. watched Nick rest his arms on the top rail and squint off into the distance, maybe studying the gathering clouds, maybe lost in the past. And suddenly she was gripped by the same restlessness as she'd felt back in the barn. Walking hadn't been enough. She blew out a swift breath. ''I want to get out of here for a while. Will you take me on the bike?''

''Where do you want to go?''

''Nowhere. Anywhere.'' She laughed shortly. ''You think we can race that storm?''

''Sounds dangerous,'' he said, coming around to face her, close enough that she felt the heat of his body and the solid beat of his heart. Not the larger than life figure of Joe's stories, but the real living, breathing Nick.

''Maybe I'm ready to take a few risks.''

His gaze narrowed on hers, causing her pulse to flutter with nerves. Then he grabbed hold of her hand and growled, ''Let's go,'' and T.C. felt anticipation gallop unfettered all over her body. Yes, she felt reckless and wildly impetuous, but more than that, she felt truly and wonderfully alive.

If T.C. had been in charge of the Ducati she would have ridden it hard into the storm, such was her mood. But Nick headed north, away from the threatening clouds.

At first the irregular acceleration as they twisted and turned through a tricky section of road honed her wildness to a sharp edge; then they hit the freeway, and the sonorous hum of the cruising engine smoothed those edges. She allowed herself to lean more deeply into the sheltering strength of Nick's body, to slide her hands into his jacket pockets and to rest her head in the hollow between his shoulder blades, which had seemingly been made for that purpose.

Instantly her mood eased from a little crazy to a lot sane. At her very core she tingled with a heightened awareness, but layered over it like the warm folds of a comfy duvet was another sensation she hadn't felt in a long time. She wrapped her arms more tightly around him and gave herself up to the feeling of absolute and total security.

They turned off the highway before they struck the border, tracking the Murray's wide river valley into the high country. Eventually they stopped at a rustic pub where they dawdled over a counter lunch and traded stories with the chatty barman.

Every so often their gazes would meet with a flash of awareness, or their knees would brush as one or the other turned on their bar stool, and the brief connection would sizzle through her blood. She was past fighting it, past analyzing it, past worrying where it might end. She simply enjoyed it.

When custom picked up, the barman drifted off and they continued to talk, skimming easily from thought to thought. He was talking about Graeme when she recalled the reason he had looked up his old friend.

"You never did tell me what you found out when you went to Melbourne."

"I found out Graeme owns a bike I covet."

She rolled her eyes. Nick grinned. Her heart rolled over.

"Okay, I found out there's nothing we can do until probate is finalized. It's a pretty complex setup, so that could take a while."

"What happens then?"

"Transmission papers are filed and the new title deed comes back in our names."

It sounded so final, so binding. A sudden anxiety churned in her stomach. "I really don't want that, Nick."

"And I don't want your half."

"Yarra Park belongs in your family," she continued doggedly.

"You want to give it to George? He'd like that. He has a buyer all lined up with a pen in his hand."

Of course she didn't want that. She didn't want anything to do with the man, especially after the things he had implied down by the track. Things she hadn't been able to walk off, or to outrun on the bike.

"What's the matter?" Nick took her hand and plaited his fingers through hers. "And don't fob me off with a 'Nothing' answer, either. I can hear the cogs turning."

"It's George. He said something earlier…"

"Did he threaten you?" His grip on her hand tightened almost painfully. "What did he say, Tamara?"

"I was too mad to make much of it at the time." She frowned, recalling the bad vibes that started afterward, as she walked Pash back to the stables. "He said I didn't belong at Yarra Park, that I should have left, and for some reason I wondered about those phone calls—if he might have been trying to scare me off, although that makes no sense. It's *you* he wants gone more than me." Spoken out loud, her concerns sounded ridiculous. She laughed self-consciously. "Forget it."

Nick didn't laugh. "He knew I'd want to sell out. You, he needed to convince."

"But those calls weren't threats, just silence." She shifted uneasily with the memory. "Why would that convince me to do anything other than not answer the phone?"

"Maybe he figured you'd be uneasy living there alone. That it would help you decide to take the money and leave." A deep frown furrowed his brow. She couldn't believe he was taking this seriously. That scared her a little. "Maybe he was building up to the threats, only then I changed the number."

"He would have been able to get the new number. Sophie did. When you've got that much money…"

He let out a long, ragged sigh. "You're right. It doesn't make sense, but then, George doesn't always function at a rational level. He proved that this morning."

"I'm probably dead wrong."

"Probably, but I'd prefer to be certain." There was a strength in the gaze holding hers, determination in the set of his jaw, and protectiveness in the hand linked with hers. He pulled her to her feet. "Come on. I'll take you home."

Nick eased the bike to a standstill inside the garage and killed the engine. Its throaty rumble continued to hum through her body, a perfect counterpoint to the rhythmic drumming of rain against the iron roof.

The storm had caught them on the road, lashing them with a cruel crosswind and buffeting squalls of rain. Despite the wild ride, despite that heart-stopping moment when the back tire lost traction on the slick bitumen, she had trusted Nick to deliver her home.

At this moment home felt like the solid strength of his big, warm body, smelled like a heady combination of wet leather and wet man. This was what she had been trying to explain that day out on the track—home wasn't so much a place as a sensation that reached inside, that took hold of your soul.

A spirit of rightness.

She felt the shifting of muscles as he lifted his arms to remove his helmet; then, in one smooth motion, he swung his leg over the tank and eased to his feet beside her. Rainwater trickled down his jacket, dripping from the hem onto jeans already so wet they were plastered to his hips and thighs. His teeth flashed white as he ripped the gloves from his hands, and something primal raced through T.C.'s blood, so hot and fast it blurred her vision.

Steady, she cautioned herself. Concentrate on *not* slithering into a boneless heap at his feet.

She focused on the zip of his jacket, then on a raindrop as it threaded its delicate path south via the jungle of metal teeth. She felt the soft scrape of his fingers against her throat as he released the clasp of her headgear, and her breathing grew shallow as he slipped the helmet from her head, unzipped her jacket and peeled it off.

"I'll get your boots. They're sodden."

"There's no need...."

"There's a need. You look like you're frozen to the seat."

She tried to move, but he stopped her with a hand on her knee, a hand so warm she swore steam rose from her wet jeans. No. She definitely wasn't frozen.

Carefully he worked the first boot off, then her thick sock. Tamara willed her senses to concentrate on something beyond the heated touch of his fingers on her ankle. Fat chance. She closed her eyes and luxuriated in the feather-soft stroke of his thumb over her anklebone. She imagined that same slow beguiling pressure elsewhere. Circling her navel. Teasing a nipple. Sliding inside her pants.

A drip of cold rainwater splashed onto the back of her neck, breaking her sensual reverie and her leaden immobility. Finally she was capable of swinging her right leg over the seat and shimmying around to sit sidesaddle.

Nick pulled the second boot off and tossed it unceremoniously behind him. Her sock followed. She noticed his eyes in the same instant that her boot thudded against the garage wall. They watched her with an intensity that would have knocked her socks off had she been wearing any.

"You need to get out of these wet jeans."

Yes, please.

The words formed, then seemed to stick somewhere between her mind and her tongue. If only she could say them. If only she could put that hand on him.

If only she weren't such a wimp.

He straightened suddenly. "You'd better go take a shower, warm yourself up. I'll see if everything's all right down at the stables."

A shower. Right. She slid to the ground, and her knees buckled, but he steadied her with firm hands.

"You *are* freezing," he murmured, and before she could reply he slipped a hand under her thighs and lifted her into his arms. The pounding rain seemed to intensify to a dull roar, although that could have been the roar of blood hammering through her veins.

The world tilted as he swung around and headed for the door, but Tamara had the distinct impression it wasn't shifting out of kilter but into perfect balance. As he struggled with the security lock, he tipped her closer to his chest, and her whole body sighed with extravagant relief. It had always known its rightful place—here, as close to Nick as the physics of matter allowed. Her slowpoke heart had taken more time to arrive at the same truth, but as he carried her inside the place she called home, it, too, caught up with the plot.

She loved him.

There was no surprise in the revelation, just a huge thickening of emotion in her chest, a complex feeling comprising as many parts pain as pleasure. She wondered if her heart was already foreseeing its broken future.

He set her down in the bathroom, on top of the vanity, and turned the shower on full steam. "Don't get out until you're properly thawed, okay?"

It was all she could do to unfurl her tongue enough to say, "Thank you."

"For?"

"Carrying me inside. Lunch. The ride."

"You had fun?"

She nodded.

One brow arched. "And I thought you said fun was overrated."

Fun. The word reverberated in T.C.'s head, seemingly in time with the water that beat against her skin. It was a timely warning, a reminder that fun was all Nick sought. Just like Miles...

No. She rejected that thought as quickly as it formed.

He was nothing like Miles. Her heart knew that truth as well as it knew the other truth. With Nick there would be no false words of love, no false promises. There would be respect and honesty, affection and attention.

Oh, and there would be heat. Firestorms of heat, for as long as this lasted.

Five days.

She had been trying not to count, trying to forget how little time was left. Only five days until he returned to New York, only five more days for her to...what?

To hesitate? To procrastinate? To hide her feelings?

Or five days to enjoy a brief taste of heaven, to embrace it with everything she felt? Could she do it? Would it be enough?

The questions pounded through her blood as she turned off the water and toweled herself dry.

What about the afterward? Could she kiss him blithely and tell him it had been fun, even while her heart was breaking?

She exited the bathroom as Nick came into the hallway from the living area. They both stopped absolutely still, her hands gripping the towel over her breasts, his fingers unbuttoning his shirt. As that first moment of stunned stillness passed, she noticed that he had shed his coat and boots, that he continued working on his shirt as he came toward her on silent feet.

That the tension in the air felt as electrically charged as the thick storm air.

In the gathering twilight gloom, she could barely make out his face. It seemed all sharp angles and shadowed planes, and with stubble darkening his jaw and his hair wildly mussed from the helmet and the rain, he looked dark and dangerous and primitive. And in that moment she knew that despite the heartache to come, despite the lack of future, she had no choice in the matter.

Her heart had made its own decision.

Weak with that knowledge, she slumped back against the wall, needing it for support, hoping it would give her strength as his gaze roamed over her flushed face, her hands gripping the top of her towel, and the length of her exposed legs beneath.

Without a word he moved past her, shedding his shirt with an almost violent shrug of his shoulders and tossing it ahead of him through the bathroom door.

So. The first move would have to be hers, and hers alone. She swallowed again. Then, with the newness of loving him full in her heart, she took that first step.

"Tight wet jeans and wet skin are a tricky combination."

He stopped in the doorway. One hand closed around the upright; the muscles across his shoulders tensed. His whole posture seemed expectant, waiting for her next words.

"You might want some help with them."

He turned, eyes glittering, a slash of color etching his sharp cheekbones. "What are you saying?"

"I'm saying I've changed my mind. And I'm asking if you've changed yours."

"Spell it out, Tamara."

Here goes nothing…and everything. She cleared her throat to make sure she enunciated each word very clearly. "Will you make love to me, Nick?"

Ten

For a long tense moment their gazes melded, his narrow, piercing, as if he needed to see into her very soul. Then he grinned, a pained lopsided quirk of the lips, but a grin all the same.

"Sure, but I'm going to need that help you offered. Feels like these jeans shrank in the rain."

"Really?"

"Why don't you come over here and see for yourself?"

Giddy with relief, with love, with nervous anticipation, she went to him. Stood close while he cupped her face in his hands and touched his lips to her forehead. The kiss was unexpectedly, exquisitely, tender. And when he breathed, "Thank God you changed your mind," T.C.'s heart swelled until she feared it would burst clean out of her chest.

Then his hands slid by her throat, over her shoulders, down her arms, and as they came to rest at her waist she imagined a faint tremor in his fingertips. She must have imagined it. Those practiced hands would never quaver.

Then he was kissing her, really kissing her. He tasted of the outdoors, chill and fresh and a little sharp, until his mouth settled more fully over hers, easing it open, and then she tasted only Nick—the absolute rightness of Nick under her lips, on her tongue, in her mouth. She could have kept on kissing him for hours—no, *days*—but then his tongue slid over hers, and the surge of desire was instant, and achingly intense.

She had to touch him, to feel him against her skin. Her hands slid around his back, urging him closer. He still wore those wet jeans, but there was nothing chilling about the contact between his powerful thighs, muscles bunched as he hunched down to her level, and her naked legs.

With a low, greedy moan she wrenched her mouth from his and buried her face in his neck. Her mouth tasted the rain on his skin; her tongue measured his rapid-fire pulse in the vulnerable hollow of his throat; her eyes drifted shut to better appreciate such a sensual smorgasbord.

His hands moved lower, cupping her hips, then lower still, until the tips of his fingers touched the backs of her thighs…and trailed a slow, deliberate course inward.

Holy jiminy! How could a touch so gentle burn as deep as a firebrand?

He eased away, and she felt the gentle tug, the drag of toweling over her skin, then nothing but cool air. The sudden chill goose-bumped her flesh, and for a moment she felt exposed and self-conscious standing naked before him. Then she heard his swift intake of breath, felt the first touch of his hands gently cupping her breasts, his dark velvet voice murmuring words of encouragement.

Eyes still closed, she felt the shift of air as he ducked his head, the cool brush of wet hair against her throat, then the rasp of whiskered skin on her breast. Her lids flew open as his tongue swirled around one fiercely distended nipple.

He drew her into his hot, moist mouth, and a tremor rippled through her body. And when he suckled deeply, hungrily, an arrow of stark desire shot straight to the core of her being.

Edgy with conflicting needs, she threaded her unsteady fingers in the cool silk of his hair, first holding him to her, then urging him away. "Let me touch you," she breathed.

"You can touch me all you like when you get me out of these cursed jeans."

She pressed herself against those cursed jeans and felt a soft shudder rack her body. Yes, it was definitely time to lose the jeans. As she reached for the button-fly, she felt his harsh inhalation, then the evidence of his desire.

Holy toledo. There was so much of him. Such a hard, pulsing, mind-blowing lot. Her head spun with an intoxicating feminine power she'd never experienced before.

Because Nick wanted her *this* much.

He drew a ragged breath. Swore softly. And suddenly he hooked his hands under her backside and lifted her. "Let's find a bed, sweet hands."

With rough impatience, he shouldered past a door. Six strides and she felt herself dropping; then the cushioning folds of soft bedcovers closed around her. By the time her head stopped spinning he had lost the jeans—without her help—and it crossed her mind that for such a leisurely man, he could move very quickly when he wanted to.

Naked at last, Nick came down to her, claiming her mouth in the way he ached to take her body, plunging his tongue between her kiss-swollen lips with undisguised hunger. He had wanted her—probably from the first touch of her hands on his body—but he hadn't counted on that desire grabbing him with vicious, clawing fingers.

Compelling him to forget slow, forget savoring the moment, forget everything other than driving himself into her heat.

Caveman tactics? Smooth, Niccolo. He hauled himself

back from the edge, slid his tongue more slowly against hers before easing away, wanting to look at her, then wanting to taste her. Everywhere. Her high, firm breasts, the curve of her belly, her soft thatch of curls. He slid a finger over her, felt her shudder, deep and strong.

"Please, Nick," she pleaded softly, her hips rolling in languid invitation.

"Yeah, sweetheart, I want that, too. Trouble is, I want everything with you, all at once." He slid a finger into her, swore urgently. "You're so wet. So tight."

Sweat broke out down his backbone as he felt her scorching heat screaming out to him. He closed his eyes, forced himself to still. He wanted to prolong the pleasure, to touch her, taste her, but when he opened his eyes, she was biting that full bottom lip, her eyes wild and hungry.

"Please, Niccolo."

Oh, man!

Protection.

He rolled with her, scrambled about in the bedside drawer, somehow managed to tear the package open and fit himself. Then he thrust into her in one long, fierce stroke, and as she closed around him, gripping him with sultry heat, he stilled, wanting to time-lock the exquisite pleasure of the moment. He gazed down into her eyes, was staggered to see tears, then humbled by the depth of wonder in her gaze. She placed a hand to his cheek and whispered, "Wow."

He had no response but to kiss away her tears. To touch her cheeks and her lashes with his lips and tongue as he started to move inside her, his strokes long and deep. He felt his control teeter when she wrapped her legs around him and tilted her hips, drawing him deeper. He moved faster, harder, compelled to completion by the rhythmical caress of her body. Then he touched her, once, and she exploded in a violent, quaking storm that shredded his control.

A savage feeling of possession burst inside him. He didn't wait; he couldn't wait. He had to pour everything of himself into her, and as she continued to pulse around him, he felt a similar clasp on his heart, squeezing him tight, as if it would never let go.

T.C. woke slowly, her brain at least a dozen steps behind her senses. They were already brimful of Nick. The steady beat of his heart against her cheek, the solid contours of his body fitted snugly against hers, the musky scent of lovemaking.

Her brain quickly found the right page.

Lovemaking...or sex? There was no doubt in her heart. In the cold morning light, she was even more in love, if that were possible. But what about Nick? Carefully she extricated herself from his arms. Had she imagined that intensity in his gaze, that feeling of once-in-a-lifetime connection? That immense sense of special?

She chewed on her bottom lip, then puffed out a breath. She had so little objectivity, and so very little experience. With a carefully covert wriggle, she put a little space between them in his big bed. Not that she was going anywhere; she just wanted some space to...look.

He lay on his side, covered to the waist. Her heart kerfudded against her ribs as she thought about pulling the sheet aside and taking her own leisurely time to drink in his beauty in the bright morning light. To look at him and maybe touch him some.

With her hands. With her mouth.

The wicked thought filled her with heat, sudden and breathtaking. How simple it would be to wriggle back over there and put her hand on his chest, to slide it over his flat hard abdomen, to lift the sheet and... She paused when voices infiltrated her secretive planning session—not the ones inside her head chanting "Go for it!" but others.

Her eyelids flew open. Had she really heard people talking? From the other end of the house came the definite sound of a door closing, and she catapulted out of the bed.

Nick rolled onto his side and regarded her with sleepy eyes. One dark eyebrow arched as he took in her flustered nakedness. "What's up?"

"You there? T.C.? Nick?"

T.C. whirled toward the open bedroom door.

"Jase," she breathed, dropping to the floor. She gathered and discarded random pieces of clothing with frantic hands, cursing when she hauled on a T-shirt back to front, fumbling to turn it around. Not an easy task when she was hunched down beneath mattress level, petrified of Jason appearing at any moment.

"He's come looking for us…. What time is it? I never sleep in…. Who else is out there? Do you have some shorts I can borrow?"

"Top drawer."

She rummaged, tugged on a pair of satin boxers, anxious eyes flicking from the door to Nick, who still lay there looking sexily rumpled and perfectly at ease. He'd probably been caught in this situation a dozen times.

"Anyone home?" This time Jason sounded closer—like out in the hallway—which meant he really was coming to find them.

"Be out in a minute," Nick called, but T.C. was already dashing around the bed and out the door.

She almost collided with Jason, whose cheerful grin froze as his eyes moved slowly from her strange attire to Nick's door, and then to some blank point on the wall behind her. His face turned a summer shade of red, which was likely a perfect match for hers. "Yesterday you said you'd be back by three, but I reckoned the storm must have held you up, so I wasn't worried. But when you weren't at the stables this morning, Mum reckoned I should come in and make sure you were all right."

"Mum?"

''She thought she'd come and see if you wanted a hand, like with the housework or anything.''

Before she could do more than issue a silent groan, she heard movement behind her, then felt the gentle weight of Nick's hands on her shoulders, easing her back against his naked chest. At least he had pulled on jeans, although he wasn't doing anything to dispel the perception of why they had slept in.

''How about you go put some coffee on, Jase? We'll be right behind you.''

They would have needed wheels and a motor to be right behind Jason, such was his haste to get away. T.C. sympathized fully. Awkward situations always made her edgy, and this rated pretty high on her personal awkward scale. What had she been thinking, lying there seducing him in her mind? She should have been aware of the time, aware that Jase would find her absence unusual.

Why *hadn't* she been thinking?

Nick smoothed his hands over her shoulders, down her arms, measuring her tension. ''You're not okay with this, are you?''

This. Great descriptive term. Covered the undefined nature of their relationship about as all-inclusively as Nick's man-size T-shirt covered her. ''No, I'm not okay, exactly.'' She blew out an unsteady breath. ''I'm embarrassed, I'm not comfortable, and I have no idea what to say or how to act.''

He pulled her resistant body to him, and his hands moved to her back, easing her closer still. Leaning on him felt very, very good. She felt his lips against her hair as he spoke to her, his voice low and soothing. ''Jase was going to find out about us whether he came into the house this morning or not, so don't make a big deal out of it. Nothing has changed. Be yourself, okay?''

No big deal? Nothing had changed? The words felt like hammer blows to her heart.

And what were you expecting, Tamara Cole? Surely, after one night, you weren't expecting words of love and promises of undying devotion? You have been there. You've heard all the pretty words, and you know exactly how casually they can be offered by a satiated man. Better to know where you stand. Better to remember that this was about fun.

That hammer kept right on, beating a tattoo on her chest.

She felt him ease back far enough to place a finger under her chin and tilt her face to meet his reassuring gaze. "Okay?"

"Okay." Somehow she managed to dredge up a smile as she stepped out of his arms. "I'd better go put some more clothes on. I think I've scared Jase enough for one day."

A shower made her feel more human, less tragic—sort of like a wet reality check. No way would Nick Corelli fall in love with her. It was hard enough adjusting to the idea of him falling in lust with her. And when she came out of her bedroom and inhaled the aroma of sizzling bacon, she forgave Jase and Cheryl their ill-timed arrival. Her grumbling stomach reminded her how, in their greedy appetite for each other, she and Nick had neglected dinner.

Later they had been too exhausted to bother.

Lost for a moment in those memories, she walked into the kitchen and straight into Cheryl's spontaneous embrace. "It's so good to see you back in this kitchen," T.C. spluttered, holding on tightly as she battled the onset of tears. After Pete's death, Cheryl had stopped working, stopped going out anywhere. This was such a positive sign.

"I thought it was time this old tart got on with life. Joe's kitchen felt like a good place to start."

T.C. hugged the other woman for a moment longer before undertaking a narrow-eyed inspection. "Hmm, you're not looking too bad for an old tart."

"And you're looking too skinny. Looks like you need a decent breakfast." With that she turned back to the frying pan, completely at home with her self-appointed task.

Smiling through her tears, T.C. poured herself a mug of coffee and looked up to find Nick watching her from the doorway, a strange expression on his face. It was impossible to describe. Intense, but not with the usual heat of lust. Definitely softer and a little...punch-drunk.

Caught off guard by the impact of that look, she sank shakily onto a stool at the breakfast bar and buried her nose in her mug. Through lowered lashes she watched him come into the room with a wink at Jason, the smooth smile as he introduced himself to Cheryl. A casual arching of one brow as he came toward her, via the coffeepot.

Consummate Nick. Obviously she'd misconstrued that look, her vision skewed by tears and the high emotion of her reunion with Cheryl.

By keeping her mouth full, she avoided participating in the conversation that flowed from today's weather—gray and gloomy with the prospect of more rain—back to yesterday's storm and on to their firsthand experience of its perils. When Nick finished his telling of their hairy trip home, Jason said, "Guess I'd better get to work, then."

T.C. started to rise, but a firm hand on her shoulder kept her in place. "No need for you to leave halfway into your breakfast. Jason can start without you."

His steady gaze challenged her to disagree.

"Start with Gina and Pash," she told Jason, although her eyes never left Nick's. "You know what to do."

The warm, steady approval in his eyes made her feel as if she had passed some kind of test. She felt inordinately pleased. Then he moved smoothly on to Cheryl, praising her cooking with a broad, white smile.

Time for another reality check, she told herself. This is Nick in full charm mode. Do not forget it.

"You want a regular spot on the payroll?" he asked Cheryl.

"One day a week would be nice. That's what I used to do for Joe."

"Done. Does your job description include shopping?"

"I noticed the cupboards were getting bare. I'll make a list."

Nick asked Cheryl if it would be easier to start an account at the supermarket or to get her a credit card; Cheryl wondered if he needed her tax number; Nick said they should discuss pay. They moved off toward the office, leaving T.C. feeling excluded and miserable.

Still, she couldn't afford to sit around feeling sorry for herself. In Nick's own words, nothing had changed. Nothing on the outside. There were horses to be exercised, boxes to be cleaned, all the things that would matter long after Nick had left.

She poured the rest of her coffee down the sink and took her miserable mood down to the stables.

Twenty minutes ago she had noticed Jason wince when he stretched to reach a saddle. Still self-absorbed, she had thought nothing of it, but this time she was standing right beside him, and the grimace on his face, quickly disguised, was undoubtedly pain.

"You've hurt yourself."

"It's nothing."

"It's not nothing if it makes your face twist in pain." He turned away, made himself busy, but she persisted, her voice full of stern authority. "Look at me, Jase."

The kid turned, face slightly flushed, eyes not meeting hers. Chastened, or still embarrassed? Hard to tell. "You think we can establish a little eye contact here?" she asked.

The pink in his cheeks deepened. She guessed embarrassment.

"Hey, Jase," she said softly. "If this is about this morning, then you've got to help me out. I'm the one caught out. I'm the one dying of embarrassment here."

"It's just...I wasn't expecting..." His gaze shifted, met hers briefly. "You know...you and Nick."

"Well, I wasn't expecting it, either."

Her wry tone stopped his nervous shuffle, and finally he met her gaze. "Do you s'pose Nick might hang around now?"

There was a hopefulness in his voice that echoed deep inside T.C. Oh, Jase, she thought, we are a fine pair, building secret expectations on a one-night stand.

Something of her thoughts must have reflected in her eyes, because Jase looked away. "Sorry. I shouldn't have said nothing. It's just been good havin' him around."

"Yes, it has. But his business is in New York. That's his life." A life as far removed from their rustic idyll socially as it was geographically. They were just a pleasant interlude, a holiday of sorts.

In the awkward, nervous silence, Jase lifted a hand to rub at his chest, and she saw the graze on his hand, the swollen knuckles.

"Your hand."

He pulled it out of sight.

"You've been fighting, haven't you?" The truth was in his eyes. "Oh, Jase. You know you can't afford to get into trouble again."

"I'm not in any trouble."

She recalled that night in the pub, Red Wilmot leaning against the jukebox and the bad feeling that had rattled through her bones. "It's Red, isn't it? Has he been giving you a hard time, because so help me if he has..."

"I can look after this myself." His jaw set stubbornly. "Geez, T.C., I already copped enough grief from Mum."

Yes, I bet you did.

She wondered if it was concern for her youngest child

that had jolted Cheryl out of her grief-imposed exile. If she was worried about Jason being led astray again by bad company. Red Wilmot was that and more. That same weird feeling gripped her again, as strong and as unfounded as her response to George yesterday, and she wondered when she had stopped thinking pragmatically and started listening to vibes.

About the same time Nick arrived to rock her rational world, she figured.

Like a thorn in her underblanket, her concerns kept nagging away long after she returned to work. The only thing that drove them completely from her mind was the sight of Nick walking toward her. At first she saw only his smile, warm enough to light both the gloomy interior of the stables and the deepest recesses of her heart.

Would she ever grow accustomed to seeing him, to the sudden breathlessness, the wild palpitations of her heart?

"Hey," he said in greeting.

"Hey, yourself."

Completely smitten, she smiled back at him. He lifted a hand, brushed something from her hair. "Straw in your hair."

A loud snort brought his attention to Star, tethered beside her. Nick leaned closer, stroked a hand the length of her sleek black neck and murmured, "Hello to you, too, beautiful."

Star flicked her ears benignly. No kicking, no head tossing, no teeth baring. Nick's brows shot up. "Would you look at that? Someone's had a change of heart."

"Maybe she's getting used to having you around."

"Is that so?" She felt his gaze resting on her face, felt her own extravagant response, and knew she would never get used to having him around.

Which was when she noticed his clothes. Crisp dark chinos, a soft fawn shirt, matching jacket. Town clothes. How could she have forgotten? One day very soon she would see him all dressed up in his town clothes, with a suitcase in each hand.

"You don't look dressed for work." She tried to smile, but it felt tight, forced.

"I'm going to Melbourne."

Was it possible to speak, to breathe, *to live,* with your heart lodged in your throat?

"I'm going to see George."

"Oh." He wasn't leaving…yet. Her heart resumed normal operations. "Is this because of what I said?"

"That's one thing." The hint of a frown touched his brow. "Yesterday I tried to talk to him, but now I realize I talked *at* him. He wasn't hearing me, and I have to make a better effort."

"And if he doesn't want to hear you?"

"Then I might have to flatten his nose again."

Aware of Jason hovering nearby, ears flapping, she shook her head. "Violence won't solve anything."

One brow arched. "Yesterday you wanted to take after him with a pitchfork."

"Not literally." She paused before plunging on. "About what I said, about the phone calls… I feel really funny about that. There's no logic to what I was thinking. You should leave it be."

With a gentle finger, he lifted her chin until she met his eyes. "I'll handle it. Trust me."

She swallowed, nodded, didn't feel a whole lot better, and she wasn't sure it was only because of the George business. Doubt bunnies were digging a huge hole in her smittenness.

"Why don't you come with me? Afterward we could have dinner somewhere."

"Like a date?"

"Yeah. Exactly like a date."

The first thing that came to mind was how she didn't have anything halfway suitable to wear, but she rejected that thought immediately. Worrying about clothes was so *not* like her. The next thing that came to mind was how the anxious churning in her gut felt as much like fear as doubt.

What on earth did she have to fear?

Not measuring up to the man at her side? Fear of falling in love with another of his many facets? Fear of facing George, knowing she had lived up to one of his snide insults? She *had* crawled into bed with her partner.

All of the above?

She shook her head, tried another of those tight, forced smiles. "It's probably a bad idea, the way George feels about me."

"That's the point. It's time he met you, sat down and talked to you. We need to clear the air."

"Can I take a rain check? I don't want to desert Cheryl on her first day back."

His gaze narrowed until she could see the light of argument in his pinpoint focus. Her agitation intensified to near panic. She did not want to go to Melbourne with him. She did not want to explain why.

Distraction seemed like the only solution.

Stretching up on her toes, she wound her arms around his neck and pressed her lips to his. It started out cool, lips to lips with a good deal of suspicion in between, but then she slid her fingers into his hair and made a low throaty you-can-do-better noise, and its whole purpose changed like wildfire. His hand closed around her nape, warm fingers that knew the exact way to touch her, and his tongue flicked against her bottom lip. Hot desire shivered into her veins, igniting her nerve endings so her skin felt too tight, her clothes harsh against her skin.

He broke it off with a low laugh that sang through her blood and rested his forehead against hers. "I gather you don't want to discuss this."

This time her smile felt natural.

"Last chance on the bike. I'm taking it back to Graeme." His hand slid down her back, pressed her closer. "We could park."

"On a bike?"

"It's a big seat. I'll manage."

She didn't doubt it, but still she straightened, touched his jaw regretfully. And shook her head.

"Jase could manage, you know that. The responsibility will do him a world of good."

"I know, but not today."

His gaze narrowed again; a frown tightened his brows. Irritated with his persistence, and more irritated with her own doubts and fears, she pulled away from him.

He took the hint.

Eleven

Despite the distraction of talking to Cheryl and worrying about Jase, the day seemed to drag on interminably. She didn't bother pretending it was for any reason other than waiting for Nick's return. She didn't bother pretending it would be any easier when he left for good. She had known that before she let herself fall in love with him.

When she couldn't stand seeing Jason hide his pain any longer—ribs, she figured—she insisted Cheryl take him to see a doctor. With twice the workload, the rest of the afternoon might prove less wearing. The phone rang around four, startling her so much she dropped a can of hoof oil. As she watched the greasy stain spread across the concrete like some brown alien slime, she wondered how long it would take before that first ring of a phone didn't lift her off the ground.

It was Nick. "Everything all right?"

"Yes."

"Are you sure?" He laughed, the sound oddly deprecating for Nick. "Forget it. I had this...feeling."

"Maybe it's catching," she murmured.

"Pardon?"

"Nothing." She twirled the cord around her hand. "How did it go? With George."

"Not so bad, considering. I don't think we'll ever be best buddies, but we made some headway." He paused, and she could picture that slight frown narrowing his gaze. "He says he knows nothing about the phone calls, and you know, I believe him. I don't know why, because he has one helluva way of bending the truth. But I do believe him on this one."

"You don't have to sound so apologetic. I told you it was only a feeling, and you've proven that they're not always reliable." She let that thought set before continuing. "There's been nothing since you changed the number, so likely it was kids. Let's forget it."

Forget it, but don't go, she willed. Stay and talk to me a while.

"You returned Graeme's bike?"

"Yeah, I'm back on four wheels."

"Damn."

"Exactly." He laughed, and she closed her eyes. Let the slow sensuous sound seep right into her, filling all those empty places. "You know you spoiled it for me."

"Me?"

"Yeah. My last ride on that beauty, and I didn't feel any of the usual. The whisper of freedom, of release. I didn't feel like I was going somewhere. I felt more like I was leaving something behind." The pause seemed chock-full of meaning, of importance. T.C. was sure her heart had stopped altogether. "I wanted you with me today."

"I know. I just... I'm sorry, Nick." She took a deep breath, wound the phone cord tightly around her fingers. "I wanted to be with you."

He swore softly, impatiently. "I'm about to leave, so I should be out there before six. You want to go somewhere for dinner?"

"We could stay in. Cheryl made something that smells like heaven."

"I'll bring wine."

"Hurry," she breathed, but she wasn't sure if he was still there. The dial tone sounded in her ear.

She showered, blow-dried her hair, slathered herself in skin lotion, even played with some makeup, although she removed most of that. She found her one set of matching underwear and agonized over clothes, eventually settling on a slinky knit top and cargoes that rode low on her hips, because, well, they were easy to get off. As far as being a seductress, it was the best she could do.

After she had set the table, she wandered about the house in an excruciating state of anticipation. Half an hour to go, even if he had heard her last urgent plea to hurry. She couldn't sit down, she couldn't stand up, and her palms were starting to sweat. In the end she took herself off to the stables, the only place likely to calm her, and as she walked the well-known path she was surprised to see a flash of movement cross the window of the tack room.

Odd. Unless Jason had come back, determined to finish cleaning today's work harness, which was exactly the kind of stunt he would pull. Shaking her head with resignation, she walked along the breezeway, calling his name.

No answer.

An uncanny warning tiptoed up her spine, and she whipped her head around, caught a flash of red hair, a twisted sneer and a raised arm. Heard two crude words, and then her head exploded in blinding white pain.

Hurry, she had breathed in that all-fire sexy voice. As if he had needed prompting. He checked his watch as the hired Land Rover bumped over the entrance grid. Grinned.

All-time new land record, Portsea to Riddells Crossing, despite stopping for wine. And flowers.

The wheels spun up gravel as he turned sharply into the yard, then lined up the garage entrance, braking sharply to park beside her Courier. He didn't know why he was in such a hellish rush. Once he was inside that door he intended to take it very slowly, and very slowly again. Maybe then they would open the wine and think about eating whatever Cheryl had cooked.

He forced himself to amble through the door. The kitchen light was on. The dining table set—with candles. "Nice touch," he murmured. Anticipation hummed through his veins as he walked the hallway. The bathroom door lay open, revealing her work clothes scattered where she had discarded them. He inhaled the lingering scent of her shampoo, pictured her naked, skin gleaming as she stepped from the water. His whole body pulsed.

Maybe the first time wouldn't be so slow.

Before he placed a hand flat against her bedroom door and watched it swing noiselessly open, he knew it would be empty. The whole house felt empty. Hollow, he realized, without her presence. He took a minute to digest the strangeness of that thought, strange because all the way back from Melbourne he had been feeling a sense of coming home. Now he was here, standing in the heart of that home, and feeling nothing but emptiness.

The stables.

He was already striding out, shouldering through doorways, and when he hit the path and heard the distant sound of Ug's shrill yapping, the anticipation in his veins turned cold with dread. He broke into a run and didn't stop until he came into the breezeway and saw her sitting there, propped against the stable wall.

"What the hell...?"

She moved her lips in a weak semblance of a smile, and

then Nick was there, hunkering down, taking her head between hands that trembled.

"Are you all right, sweetheart?"

"My head...exploded," she mouthed.

He looked into her glassy eyes, saw the flash of pain when his fingers tightened involuntary. Swore silently. "I'm sorry, baby." He swung her into his arms, and her head lolled against his chest.

She murmured "Better," and for a minute he couldn't move with the tremendous weight of relief.

She was all right. A concussion, he figured, but he was taking her straight to casualty to make sure.

Halfway to the hospital she turned toward him and said very lucidly, "I know who it was. I saw him."

If people didn't stop treating her like an invalid, she would scream...well, maybe not scream, since her head was still inclined to ache, but she would definitely whisper in a loud, aggravated tone. When the hospital released her after overnight observation she had breathed one mighty sigh of relief, but now she'd been home two days and it was worse than ward four.

Tired of her own company and daytime television, she had ventured down to the stables. Nick had picked her up and carried her back here, muttering something about her not knowing how to stop working.

"I had a bump on the head. I'm over it."

"Is it so hard to let someone look after you?"

He had been so angry that she'd let it be. Last night he'd insisted she sleep in her own bed, alone, which hadn't done anything for her head except make it spin with paranoia. Maybe that one night hadn't been as wondrous for him as for her. Maybe her encounter with the rough end of a shoeing rasp had provided Nick with the perfect out. Maybe one night was all she would have.

The notion had transfixed her with paralyzing force, so

when he'd come to say good-night, when he'd leaned down to kiss her lips with heartbreaking gentleness, when she'd longed to rope her arms around his neck and draw him down beside her, she had lain motionless and said nothing lest she blab about staying and loving her, not just for this night but forever.

When she woke, he had gone down to the stables, returning just before the police came to tidy up their investigation. They'd arrested Red the night he attacked her, and with several thousand dollars worth of Yarra Park harness in his trunk, he had little comeback. Drunk, belligerent and at odds with the world, he confessed to everything, including the phone calls.

That had started out as a drunken game aimed at unsettling the woman he blamed for turning Jason against him. The thought of robbery had just started to take shape when Nick answered the phone, putting him on the back foot. A woman on her own was the perfect prey for a coward like Red Wilmot.

After his fight with Jason, he had been seething with the need to retaliate, and he'd lucked out when he overheard Nick tell the service-station attendant he was heading into Melbourne for the day. He waited, watched and struck after T.C. went back to the house at the end of her day's work.

If she hadn't happened along when she did, he might just have taken what he came to get—anything portable and salable—or he might have had his fun trashing the place and turning the horses loose. He had done a little of that, she gathered, although both Nick and Jase shrugged it off as minor.

Don't you worry your poor aching little head about it, was the tenor of their response to her questions.

Now the police were long gone, and she had woken from an afternoon nap to find Cheryl had also left. She was alone, bored and gnashing her teeth. Somewhere in the distance thunder grumbled in sympathy, and she wandered onto the verandah to watch the approaching storm. A portentous bank of deep gray hung over the southern hills, split suddenly by a flash of lightning.

Had it been only three days since the last storm? It felt like so much longer.

The wild spirit of that day hovered around her, melding with her restless mood, until she grabbed her wind-cheater and took off at a brisk walk. This time she thought about her route, choosing a path that circled the property with an added loop along the river bank. At the farthest point the wind shifted without warning, blustering in from the south, and she knew she was about to get wet.

That didn't bother her. Instead she stopped to hold her arms wide and lift her face to the first heavy drops of moisture. With her eyes closed, the rain seemed to fall in slow motion. A plop on her forehead. A second striking the point of her chin and rolling down her throat. The next came in twin splashes on her cheeks, and then the heavens opened with a deafening roar.

A shout of laughter burst from her open mouth as she twirled in a wide circle and started to run. How long had it been since she had taken the time to run in the rain? Usually she was running *from* the rain, bustling to finish some chore or other, too busy to appreciate the freshness in the air, to breathe the rich scent of damp earth, or to jump the rivulets that trickled across the road. The other day she had wanted to outrace the storm; today she wanted to run with it.

By the time she collapsed on the edge of the verandah, she was panting hard from exertion. Behind her, the screen door opened, then clattered shut. She heard the firm tread of boots and smiled broadly as she straightened out of her restorative head-between-knees posture.

"Thank you," she managed to breathe as she looked up

past the denim legs and chambray work shirt into his set
expression.

"What the hell have you been doing?"

Her smile froze. "Taking a walk. I needed the air."

"Couldn't you see it was going to storm?"

"It came in quicker than I thought." She laughed a
little, determined not to let his attitude faze her. "Isn't it
glorious?"

"What it is, is dangerous. You better get inside and out
of those wet things."

"I am a bit soaked, aren't I?"

She felt the touch of his gaze as it flicked over her, but
his mouth didn't lose its hard set. "If you hate being an
invalid so much, you'd better get out of those clothes."

"I'll drip water all through the house."

"It'll survive."

Now he was starting to steam her, standing there with
that grim look on his face. What had happened to the old
Nick? The one with the easy smile and laid-back attitude.
Poetry in slow motion, she'd labeled him that first day.
Now he reminded her more of a funeral dirge.

"Come on, Tamara. Quit mucking about and get out of
those wet things."

"Okay," she said affably, and she started undoing buttons. Her jacket came first, peeled off and dropped to the
ground in a sodden heap. Next she wrenched off her boots,
her socks. She had managed the pull her shirt out of her
jeans when strong hands lifted her, swung her up and
around in the one economical motion.

Déjà vu.

Except this time she didn't stop herself from looping
her arms around his neck and angling her body closer to
his. He stopped in his tracks, and as quick as a clash of
lightning across the storm-darkened sky, the mood
changed. She felt it in his extreme stillness, broken only
by the small movement in his throat as he swallowed.

"I'm still furious, you know."

She smiled. "I know."

Twisting a little, she tried to see his face, but it was impossible from this angle.

"It was getting late. I didn't know where you'd gone." His arms tightened around her in strong contrast to the concern that softened his voice. Her heart bounded, lodged in her throat, and something hummed vaguely around the edges of her memory, something else he'd said that had caused the same leap of hope. Something about leaving her behind. She wished she could remember....

"What were you thanking me for?"

"Pardon?"

"On the verandah, when you came out of the rain."

"Oh. I wanted to thank you for making me stay home, for slowing me down and giving me the opportunity to run in the rain."

Said out loud, it sounded a bit loopy, until he bent his head and she felt a smile in the kiss he pressed to her forehead. "You're welcome."

He held her easily in one arm while he opened the door, but the redistribution of weight brought her breasts into contact with the hard wall of his chest. They responded immediately, hardening, shooting desire into the depths of her body, and she wanted no impediment, no barrier. She wanted to be skin to skin.

Impatiently she grabbed his shirt, pulling at the buttons and silently bemoaning her clumsiness. As he maneuvered them through the door a button popped free, then a second, and she slid her hand inside to rest against his heartbeat momentarily before moving restlessly on, touching the fine smattering of hair, measuring its harsh texture over the smoothly muscled flesh beneath, sliding over a nipple and back again.

One bare foot swung down and skimmed the front of his fly. His extremely distended fly. He stopped stock-still in the center of the kitchen as she pressed her bare toes against him, as her whole body shimmered with heat.

He drew a harsh breath. "Easy, sweetheart, there's no rush. If you keep that up, I won't get past the table."

T.C. imagined the glossy patina of polished cedar sliding against her naked skin and gave a dreamy little shiver of pleasure. "And that's a problem?"

He laughed softly as he resumed walking, the fall of his boots loud against the slate floor. For the boots of a man urging *her* to slow down, they seemed to be moving in a mighty big hurry. She smiled her approval as he carried her into his room and lowered her to his dresser.

"These wet jeans will have to go." His words were a statement of fact, but his voice…oh, the glorious things that dark velvet voice could do. Then his hands skimmed under her shirt, his long fingers tucking into the waistband of her jeans. The pleasure reached so deep she swore it stroked her very soul, and she knew only Nick had the power to touch her so deeply.

She smiled a siren's smile. "Be my guest."

His eyes darkened as he unsnapped the waistband and eased the zip open. Then the back of his hand brushed against her bare belly, and her swift intake of breath sounded loud and harsh. He drew back a fraction, so when he touched her again it wasn't only with his hand. She felt the heated caress of his gaze trailing his fingertips as they dipped into her navel, as they pressed lightly against the soft curve of her belly, as they slid lower to trace the lace banding her bikini panties.

A delicious heaviness pooled low in her body and flowed through her like liquid heat. Her throat closed around a soft moan—of pleasure, encouragement, hunger—as she willed those teasing fingers to push away the scrap of material, to touch the core of her need, so hot and wet and demanding.

Oh, how she craved that touch.

"Lift up," he growled suddenly, startling her out of her sensual lethargy. Obediently she lifted her backside so he could peel the wet denim over her hips and down her legs.

Then he picked her up again, lowered her to his bed. Eyes closed, she heard a click she recognized as the lamp.

"Hell," he swore softly. "The storm must have knocked the power out."

"We need power because...?"

"It'll be dark soon." He touched the backs of his fingers against her cheek. "And I want to be able to see your face when I'm inside you."

The words, spoken so slowly, softly, definitely, painted the most erotic images. Her fingers curled instinctively, gripping the covers. "There are candles," she managed to say. "In the pantry."

"Perfect." He ran his knuckles lightly over her cheek again, her softly parted lips, whispered, "Don't move," and headed for the door.

"Hurry back."

She felt his eyes on her, burning her. "Oh, I'm running."

With a frustrated groan, she turned her face into the covers. Closing her eyes, she rubbed her cheek languidly against the cool, crisp linen, nostrils flaring as she inhaled his scent. She stretched her limbs and frowned when her rucked-up shirt tightened uncomfortably across her shoulders. God, her shirt... She fumbled with the buttons, tearing one off in her haste to rid herself of the cumbersome old thing.

"Tip one in seductive technique. Lose the flannel work shirt," she muttered as she tossed it aside, revealing her plain practical cotton chemise.

For the first time in her life she wished for lacy, diaphanous underwear of the kind Nick would be used to. Exotically scented skin and voluptuous breasts to fill the lacy, diaphanous underwear would be nice, too, but she saved her breath on wishing for them. And oh, for the confidence to strip, to arrange herself artfully on his bed wearing nothing but a sultry come-hither smile.

Her decidedly unsultry snort of laughter destroyed that image. "Who am I kidding?" she muttered.

Tamara Cole doing sultry was as likely as Tamara Cole enticing Nick to stay, and for all the heat in his eyes, for all his concern and caring these past few days, Nick was leaving. The knowledge should have cooled her ardor, but it didn't, for she knew that loving Nick, even for this brief time, would be worth the heartache that followed.

He returned on silent feet, and she sensed him moving around the bed, heard the faint clunk of a candleholder placed on the bedside table, then the scratch of match against flint. The distinctive smell of burning candlewick reached her nostrils a second before she opened her eyes to find him standing over her, his eyes glittering with golden shards of reflected candlelight.

Such a beautiful man. Far too beautiful for her.

She eased herself forward and sat on her haunches on the very edge of the bed. Then she looked way, way up. What she saw there made her weak and strong at once. His eyes had fastened on her breasts, on the nipples she felt budding tightly against her chemise, and they smoldered with banked heat. His nostrils flared, and he swore softly, almost reverently, as his gaze slid back to hers.

The air seemed to thicken with sultry heat; her whole body vibrated with it. Her focus narrowed to this moment, to the image of her and Nick isolated from the rest of the world by the rain that cloaked the house like a thick gray curtain, and even more by the strength of their desire.

Breathing heavily, she lowered her gaze to his bare chest, then tracked the dark hair that arrowed down to his jeans. She sat back on her heels and ran her tongue around her dry mouth. Oh boy, she wanted to touch him. Right there, where his jeans stretched so tautly. The need prickled in the palms of her hands.

"It's time you delivered on that offer, Tamara." God, how she loved the way her name rolled from his tongue. She closed her eyes and let the lush syllables wash over her. "Take my jeans off."

His hands cradled her face for a moment, then slid into her hair, drawing her closer to all that broad, hard man.

"Okay," she breathed, "but first I have to touch you."

"Be my guest," Nick murmured, but his attempted grin felt tighter than a grimace, and at the first tentative touch of her hand he damn near rose off the floor. It was no more than a brush of fingertips against denim, but he hauled in a tight breath and told himself to get a grip. The caress of a woman's hands was one of life's greatest joys, and on the joy-scale, Tamara's touch equated to pure ecstasy. Not pain, he lectured himself as her fingers spread over his stomach.

So why did that almost shy caress cause his chest to feel as if it was being gripped in some giant vise?

He heard her draw a tremulous breath before sliding her palms to his waist and up his sides. Her thumbs traced the line of his bottom rib, then hesitated again. His whole body screamed in need. It felt as if every cell was clamoring for her attention, until he could no longer stand the suffocating tension. His eyes flashed open and focused over her head—on her reflection in the mirrored wardrobe door.

The candlelight danced over her as she knelt before him, a burnished canvas of shadow and pale shimmering light. From her golden halo of hair down the long straight line of her back, from the dip of her waist to the feminine fullness of her buttocks, her beauty stunned him. Nick hadn't actually run to get the candles, yet that picture caused his chest to ache as if he'd covered the distance at world-record pace. At altitude.

"Beautiful," he murmured, his voice so husky it was barely audible.

She shook her head.

"Yes. You are incredibly, amazingly," he pressed his lips into her soft hair, "arousingly beautiful."

Her expressive sigh whispered against his chest as his hands slid onto her delicate nape. *Delicate.* He smiled at the unbidden description. His strong, independent Tamara wouldn't like it. His hands slid over her shoulders and down her arms, taking the straps of her chemise with them. As he peeled the thin garment from her skin, he heard the sharp little hitch of surprise in her breath and knew he'd uncovered her breasts. That she sat before him bare to the waist.

He didn't look.

Resolutely he concentrated on the erotic image in the mirror. His hands slowly skimming the length of her arms and back again. His hands so big and dark as they spanned her waist. His fingers playing along her spine, pushing under her rolled-down top and into those sexy little dimples above the curve of her buttocks.

Then he felt her hands on him, sliding from his chest to below his navel. He fisted his hands in her hair as if that might help him hold on to his thin thread of control. His absolute concentration on their reflection had somehow removed him from the present, or from his body, but the touch of her fingers brought him back to the here and now with a clattering force.

He forced his hands to gentle, to ignore his rampant need to haul her forward. The very thought caused him to pulse with a hardness akin to pain. She touched him again, tracing his length with a fingertip he shouldn't have felt through the thickness of denim. But he felt it, all right, like a scorching fire-trail.

"Take them off, Tamara."

Ignoring his tight-lipped demand, she touched him more

boldly, and when he caught the look in her eyes, of awe, fascination, excitement, his knees almost buckled. When she wet her lips, Nick groaned violently and jammed his eyes shut.

Momentarily her hands left him. Then she started to pull his jeans down, leaning forward for more purchase. She was so close that he could feel her breath on his skin. A wisp of hair brushed the inside of his thigh, and his hands clenched into tight fists to stop himself from dragging that warm, moist mouth to him.

Hell, if he allowed her that, that lush mouth closing over him, he wouldn't last beyond the first sweet touch of her tongue. The thought wrenched a tortured sound from his throat, and she sat back on her heels.

"Sorry," she breathed, her big eyes staring up at him, her teeth biting down on her bottom lip, and such a look of remorse on her face.

"Oh please, sugar, don't ever be sorry for making me feel like this."

He reached for protection, held it out for her. "You want to do this?"

And oh man, she did it so well.

He struggled to slow his hands, hands too eager to strip the rest of her clothes from her body. In one motion he peeled both pieces of underwear over her hips and down her legs, legs that trembled under his touch. Her beauty stunned him anew as his hands and eyes and mouth skimmed over her nakedness, loving the lushness of her mouth, the length of her neck, the soft flesh of her inner thighs, and those breasts, even more perfect than he'd remembered.

With one hand splayed across her belly and his mouth at her breast, he stroked her sensitive swollen bud with light sureness, teasing her and pleasing her until she whimpered and arched and cried out to him. For him. Only then did he give her what she craved, first with his mouth; then, while the cries of release still broke from her, he lifted her hips and drove himself home.

Home. Not a place but a woman.

A woman of satin skin and tender hands, of lean strength and soft curves, of immense strength and fragile ego. A woman whose sultry heat drew him deeper into her body while her heat-hazed eyes drew him deeper into her soul. A woman whose soft keening moans drove him higher and harder until pleasure burst, pure and true, in a Technicolor shower of sensation that spiraled out of control, even as her name exploded from his lips.

Tamara.

Spent, he sank into her curves, covering her with his body, fingers entwined, foreheads touching, limbs aligned.

He was home.

Twelve

One candle burnt out before Nick could move. The rain had stopped, and he supposed it would be dark but for the weak glow of the remaining flame. Following the rain, it would be cold outside, but here in his bed it was warm, thanks to the woman in his arms.

Bathed in flickering light, she lay limp and satiated, her face nestled between his shoulder and chin, her legs still intertwined with his amid the tangle of sheets. He smiled and pressed his lips to her forehead, traced a finger down the line of her nose. She murmured something sleepily that might have been his name, and the soft, sweet sound whispered across his skin and eased its way into his heart. His arms tightened around her, held her more closely.

The woman he loved.

He lay perfectly still and absorbed the intense sense of satisfaction the knowledge brought...and wondered when his hunger for her had ceased to be merely a painful groin-based one and spread to fill his whole being. He wanted to wake her, to tell her. He wanted to see that sunrise smile spread across her face as she heard those three little words.

Words he had never before thought, let alone uttered.

Except that this was Tamara, and there was no guarantee she would accept his love easily or quickly. What was it she had said down at the stables? *It could take months for a temperament like hers to come around.* He'd known then, as he knew now, that it wasn't Star's disposition in question.

No, he needed to be patient and careful in handling Tamara. He needed to ease her into the notion, to give her time to arrive at the truth herself. Problem was, he didn't have the luxury of time, not with his return to New York only days away.

Something twisted tight in his gut when he thought about leaving her, as he remembered his fear when he'd found her in the stables, and again when he had come home to an empty house this afternoon.

The solution seemed simple. She would come to New York with him. Together they would do what had to be done to pack his things, to sort out his business; then, together, they would return to Yarra Park.

It sounded simple, but nothing was really ever simple with Tamara.

"Come with me."

The hand resting languidly on his chest tensed. "To New York?"

"Yes." He slid down the pillow, turned his head to better see her face. "I don't want to leave you here alone."

She traced the line of his collarbone with one gentle finger. "I have a dog and twenty-three horses. I'm never alone."

"Okay. Then, how about I don't like being alone?"

"Alone in New York? Now there's a novel concept!"

Nick didn't smile.

"You're serious." She rolled onto her back and let go her breath in a long, serious-sounding way. It made Nick hold his own breath. "What would I do over there while you're working? You know how I can't stand doing nothing. And I really hate cities."

"You hate being out of your comfort zone."

As soon as he said it, Nick regretted it. He saw her tense, felt her withdraw another notch. *Hell.* He needed to do better, much better.

"Remember I said I needed to be back by the twenty-fifth?" He waited for her small nod of acknowledgment. "There's a fund-raiser the next week for a charity I support."

"What kind of a charity?"

"A foundation to help disadvantaged kids. It relies heavily on this annual bash for its running costs. This isn't something I can miss, Tamara, and I want you there, too."

A mixture of curiosity and apprehension, a hint of yielding, softened the green of her gaze. Nick smiled. This was better.

"It's a dinner and an auction, and a few celebrities always turn up."

"Sounds like a big deal."

"It is for the foundation. But for you, green eyes, it'll be fun. What do you say?"

Wrong choice of argument. Nick saw it in her face a full second before she shifted her head on the pillow in silent rejection.

"Do me a favor and think about it, okay?"

This time she shook her head more resolutely. "I won't change my mind."

"You want to tell me why?"

She fixed him with those big expressive eyes. "You remember the Tamara you described to me, down at the stables one day? The one in the floaty dress and the heels and the perfume? Well, *she* is the kind of girl you would take to a New York fund-raiser, not me.''

"It's you I'm asking.''

"I'm sorry, Nick.''

She turned away, her chin set in that inflexible way he had come to recognize. But then he considered her curiosity about the foundation and his own determination. Just like the horse she called Star, Tamara needed time and the right kind of handling. He still had a couple of days to work on her, and, just like Star, she would come around to his way of thinking.

The next afternoon he was closeted in the office trying to catch up on some of his recent neglect. Both mind and body wanted to be elsewhere, and while he could park his body in a chair and tell it to stay put, he couldn't stop his mind from wandering.

Its natural inclination was to wander all over the past thirty or so hours and the fact that he hadn't been able to change Tamara's mind. Perhaps he shouldn't be pushing the fund-raiser thing, but, hell, he wanted her there. Tonight may well be his last chance to talk her into it.

If he couldn't change her mind, then it would be one of his last nights with her for weeks...at least two, maybe three, maybe more. Either way, tonight had to be special.

The idea grabbed such a firm hold that he didn't hesitate before calling Sophie. He wanted the best, and Sophie knew nothing else. To hell with any consequences.

It was coming up to five when Tamara stuck her head in the door. "I have to go pick up some feed. Want to come?''

"Do you have to leave right away? I have to finish this report.''

She came in and sat on the edge of his desk. "Type quickly. The feed store closes at five-thirty.''

While he labored at the keyboard, she picked up a slip of paper. Sophie's restaurant list, he noticed, wishing he had put it out of sight. He wanted this to be a surprise.

"Ooh, fancy," she commented with a hint of a smirk.

"You know these places?"

"I know *of* them. They're hardly the kind of places I'd *know* know."

He lifted a brow.

"These are the kind of places where they check the labels on your clothes to make sure you can afford the prices, which, incidentally—" she leaned toward him as if confiding some great secret "—they don't put on the menus."

Nick didn't return her smile. "I can afford their prices."

"Hey, I know that, although I can't see why you bother. The food's overrated." She gave a dismissive little shrug as she put the list down. "Now, are you coming to town? We could grab a pizza from Dom's."

"I gather they're neither overpriced nor overrated?"

She blinked, looked a little confused by his terse answer. "No, *and* you don't have to dress up."

Nick knew he should leave it there, but he couldn't. He leaned back in his chair and regarded her through narrowed eyes. "How is it you know so much about these fancy restaurants if you've never been to one?"

"I didn't say that. I only said I haven't been to these particular ones." She slid from the desk, her face blank of all expression. "I have to go if I'm going to catch Weale's."

"Hang on a minute." Nick was on his feet, a hand wrapped around her arm before she could take another step. "We haven't finished this discussion."

"First you'll have to tell me what the discussion is about."

"What it *is* about," he ground out, "is a date. You and me."

"Oh."

He studied her for a second, the slight flush in her cheekbones, the strangely vulnerable look in her eyes.... With a muttered oath he pulled her into his arms. She came, stiff and resistive. Unyielding. "I'm leaving the day after tomorrow, and I want to take you out somewhere nice."

"You don't have to do that. I like Dom's pizza."

Her hands pushed against his chest, forcing him to release her. That bit at the already frayed edges of his temper. "That's not the point."

"What *is* the point, Nick?"

"The point is... *hell!*"

The point was, he needed tonight. He needed to show her what he couldn't tell her. That he loved her, respected her, wanted a relationship with her. That he wanted to do things for her, to cosset her, to protect her. That he wanted her with him... beside him.

"I want you to come to New York."

He hadn't meant to say that, not so forcefully. She actually took a step backward, then another. And for once the expression on her face, in her eyes, gave no clue as to what was going on in her mind. He felt a chilling sense of dread deep in his gut as she took a long, measured breath.

"Don't you think it's best if we leave it here?"

The dread turned icy in Nick's veins. For the first time it struck him that she might not share his feelings about their relationship. That she might be happy to wave him goodbye. That this might have been only about sex... or about softening him up. To get her way with Yarra Park.

"You want to expand on that?" he asked, and his voice sounded about as cold as he felt.

"Look, Nick, it's been nice, and as you said, fun."

"Spare me the platitudes. You've been using me? Is that what you're saying?"

Taken aback, maybe by his words, maybe by the sharpness of his tone or the harshness he felt in his expression, she shook her head almost fiercely. "No."

He watched her face as she struggled to make sense of his accusation.

"Are you saying I slept with you to change your mind about the inheritance?" she asked slowly.

"Did you?"

Wariness returned, wariness and uneasiness, peeping out at him from between her thick lashes, and Nick laughed harshly. He didn't want to hear her answer, not if it wasn't honest.

"Forget it. It doesn't make a lick of difference to my decision," he said.

"You have decided?"

"Yes." Nick couldn't remember when he'd reached that decision. Maybe he hadn't until this moment. "I'm keeping my half, but I'm not taking what's been given to you. If you want your name off that deed, then you can take the money I offered you for it."

He turned to the desk and scribbled out a check.

"This is for your half of the land. We'll have to work out a better valuation on the horses. I don't believe the one the solicitors gave me is fair."

She didn't take it from his outstretched hand. Her face was very pale as she shook her head slowly, a little stunned. "I don't want your money."

He tossed the piece of paper on the desk. "Then give it to charity."

As they stood there facing each other in that strange state of standoff, the cold infiltrated Nick's bones. He could talk all night long, but he wouldn't change her mind—not about picking up that check, not about coming to New York, not into believing they had a future.

"Hell, you could give stubborn lessons to a mule."

"I'm not trying to be difficult." Her eyes pleaded with him to understand. "You know how I feel about this."

"You want to have another try at explaining? Because I don't believe I do. I don't believe you've ever told me the full story about anything. About how you came to work for Joe and why it meant so much to you. About why Joe left you a piece of this place. About why you slept with me, or about why you won't come to New York."

He stared at her for a moment, as she stood there wearing her tough, insular, independent armor, but with some kind of silent plea in her eyes. He knew he only had to open his arms and she would be there, but he also knew if he didn't stand tough, she would never talk to him. Never tell him the whole story.

"I'll be catching the earliest flight I can get a seat on tomorrow. You want to talk between now and then, you know where to find me."

T.C. did find him the next morning, down at the barn, standing outside Star's stall. With her pulse thumping double time, she stilled to watch him, to drink in the completeness of his male beauty. He was everything she wanted in a man, everything she longed to hold in a man...but could she tell him?

Heart in mouth, she watched Star's tentative approach, saw the mare hesitate, head lowered but steady. No head tossing, no eye rolling, no foot stomping. It would take nothing more than a few words of reassurance, a certain tone of voice and a confidence-giving straight look, and she would come to him, put herself in his hands.

Silently she willed him to extend his hand, to say those words, to make it easy. But he stepped away, turned and moved on to the next stall.

Saying his goodbyes.

The reality of the moment rocked her to her very core. He was about to leave. This was her last chance to speak her heart. Oh, she longed to lay it all out for him, all those true stories he had encouraged her to tell, yet he had given so little away, had admitted nothing of his feelings for her. And she still felt so much like a first starter tossed into a match race with a stakes champion.

If only he had turned and found her standing there. If only he had offered some word of encouragement, some sign. If only he had come and kissed her in that way he had, that way that made her feel as if *she* were the champion.

But he kept on walking out the far end of the barn. She took a deep breath and found the air rich with leather and horsehair, sweet molasses and fresh clover hay...and found none of her usual bracing reassurance in the familiar scents.

She wondered if she ever would again.

Life after Nick left was exactly as T.C. had expected. Hollow, colorless, lonely, as gray as the skies that kept her misery company. Even Cheryl's fresh batch of double choc-chip muffins was doing little to lift her spirits.

"Something on your mind?" Cheryl asked.

Not on my mind, on my heart. "This ugly weather's getting to me."

"Only the weather?" Cheryl shook her head, a soft smile of understanding on her lips. "You miss him. It's okay to admit it."

"That's ridiculous. He's only been gone a few days."

"A few days is a long time when you're in love."

T.C. laughed softly, self-consciously. "Is it so obvious?"

"To another woman." She paused tellingly. "Have you told him?"

"Three weeks ago he was just a larger-than-life character in Joe's stories."

"I knew Pete was the one after two hours."

"Really?"

"We met on holiday in Queensland, and that first day I didn't know anything about him other than how he made me feel. Turned out we lived at opposite ends of the country, and we both had our families there, our lives. When I went home, I was so miserable I knew I had to do something about it."

"What did you do?"

"I gave notice at work and started packing all my things, and then Pete turned up at my door. He had fewer things to pack."

"I couldn't go to New York. I couldn't live there."

"Did he ask you to?"

T.C. shook her head. "He asked me to go with him, to be his date at this charity thing."

"And let me guess—you turned him down cold?"

"I couldn't just leave on a few days' notice."

Cheryl lifted her brows. "You could've if you'd wanted to. You know Jase and I would have managed, or you could have got someone in to help out—old Harry or Gil's brother."

"But I don't know how he feels about me, what he expected of me if I went to New York. I couldn't put myself through that. Not again."

"Nick's not like that other bastard."

"I know, but he could hurt me so much worse."

"Oh, sweetie." Cheryl came to her then, embraced her with arms full of compassion and reassurance. "There's lots of things hurt, but you know what hurts most? Regrets."

A thick haze of tears clouded Cheryl's eyes as she released T.C. She wiped them unselfconsciously on the edge of her apron.

"I've been pretty miserable this past year, and it's only been the kids that have kept me sane, them and the memories of all the happy times me and Pete had together. You don't want to grow old with only regrets. Memories make much better company.''

T.C. shifted restlessly on her stool. "Are you saying I should go over there?''

"You make up your own mind on that, but I *am* telling you it's time you stopped looking behind you and started looking toward your future.''

"If only it were that easy," T.C. said heavily. "But we were never starting from scratch.''

"What do you mean?''

"Joe left me a letter to explain his will. He wasn't only giving me half of Yarra Park. He was giving me Nick.''

"Matchmaking.'' Cheryl shook her head, then chuckled with rich amusement. "And doesn't that sound just like Joe?''

"Yes, but strangely enough, I can't see the funny side. I don't want the inheritance or Joe's matchmaking or anything else between us. I just want it to be about him and me.''

"I take it you never explained this to Nick?'' Cheryl regarded her through shrewd eyes. "And why not? He's a good man, sweetie. You should talk to him.''

"I know he's a good man, Cheryl, but how do I know I'm a good enough woman for him?''

"Joe must have thought so. He picked you out for his favorite son.''

Sure, Joe might have thought so, but Joe had been biased. How long could she hold the interest of a man who craved excitement and challenge? Whose life was devoted to moving from one adventure to the next?

She wanted Joe to be right. She wanted Nick, but she wanted to hold him for life, not just until he moved on.

As she selected a search engine, T.C. told herself she was doing the research out of interest. She simply wanted to know more about this charity Nick supported.

The Alessandro Foundation.

After a frustrating ninety minutes she stumbled across it in a magazine article, and as the facts unfolded line by line, she found herself creeping closer and closer to the computer screen, drinking in every snapshot of the boy Nick had been and a new understanding of the man he had become.

She saw a young Nick in the character sketches of the youths the foundation helped. Kids they took from a dead-end existence to places and experiences they could never have known existed. Wilderness camps and cattle drives, kayaking trips and mountain climbs, places that would challenge their boundaries, tackling tasks that would build their self-esteem.

The foundation aimed to prove that, with courage and commitment and a positive attitude, they could do things they'd never dreamed possible.

T.C. sat back in her chair. The kind of courage and commitment and positive attitude she needed to go after her future.

Without looking any further, she knew Nick's involvement far transcended that of a passive supporter. She knew why he had undertaken so many adventure expeditions over the past years, why he had been in Alaska when Joe died, and her heart tightened painfully in her chest.

How could she have so misunderstood him?

How could she not have seen the man he was?

It was a long time before she could go on, searching with more purpose now, needing to find out about the charity auction, if there was still time to do something that would take courage, that would show commitment and strength of character.

Something that would take her way outside her comfort zone. But if she succeeded, if she could do this, maybe she would also have proved to herself that she was worthy of Nick.

Thirteen

Finding out about the fund-raiser was the easy part. Finding out that Nick was the prime lot, that a gaggle of rich, beautiful and savvy women would be bidding for a weekend adventure with him as their private guide...that was the hard part.

Because she knew instantly what she had to do.

She picked up the check Nick had tossed on the desk, and the sight of all those zeros caused her eyes to cross.

"You said to give it to charity. I suppose it might as well be your favorite one."

Resolutely she folded the check and tucked it into her pocket; then she leaned back in her chair to consider the practicalities. They were so much easier to focus on. She had two days. No, a day more, she realized, thinking about the time difference between the two continents. She blew out a long breath and tried to ignore how it quavered.

Not much time, and beyond booking a plane ticket, she didn't know where to start. If she called, Nick would either

arrange everything or he would tell her not to bother.
And/or he would demand to know why she had changed
her mind, why she was coming. He would demand to hear
all those full stories.

He would have them soon enough, but not over the
phone. This was about proving her love, about proving
herself worthy. It was not a coward's task and would not
be done the coward's way. No, sirree.

She pictured the stunned silence in the room when she
made her bid, the spotlight falling on a lone woman...a
small blonde wearing the wrong kind of dress and tripping
over heels she couldn't manage. For a moment her resolve
weakened. Those old insecurities clawed their way back
to the surface and dug in with sharply honed talons.

They screeched, *Remember your last sad attempt at so-
phistication? Miles laughing as he told you to stick to your
boots. Remember the patronizing laughter of his friends?*

And then she remembered the look in Cheryl's eyes
when she spoke of regrets. No, she didn't want to grow
old with regrets. She wanted a chance at the memories.

She slapped her hand down on the desk with a purpose
that belied the enormity of what she still had to do. Get
her hands on a ticket to a fancy New York society fund-
raiser, get herself to that city, find something to wear.

Fifteen minutes later, she heard a car pull up.

A compact European sedan sat in the drive, and when
T.C. came out the door, a vaguely familiar looking woman
slid out of the driver's seat and pushed designer shades to
the top of her sleek dark bob.

"Hello, you must be Tamara." She smiled across the
roof of her car. "I had to come and meet you. Curiosity
is my middle name. That makes me Sophie *Curiosity* Corelli."

She came around the car, at least five foot eight of elegant taste and exquisite grooming, and extended a per-

fectly manicured hand. T.C. took it in her smaller unmanicured one. "Hello, Sophie. I've heard a lot about you."

Both perfectly shaped brows shot up. "Is that so?"

T.C. felt a betraying warmth in her cheeks. Sophie *Troublemaker* Corelli, Nick had called her. The sister with too much time on her hands. She glanced down at Sophie's Italian sandals, then up at her artfully applied makeup. She couldn't recall praying for a fairy godmother, but it seemed as if one had arrived behind the wheel of an Audi 4.

"Would you like a coffee?" she asked with a tentative smile.

"No, but I'd kill for something cold."

T.C. took a deep breath and ushered the woman she hoped to make her ally into the house.

Two nights later, she stood trembling in the lobby of one of Manhattan's most exclusive restaurants, wondering what had possessed her to undertake such a foolhardy scheme. Slinking away and leaving the country undetected suddenly seemed mighty appealing.

Is that what you really want? Is that why you went through all that tedious primping and preening? The hairdresser and the beautician and the exhausting shopping trip? If you chicken out now, how will you face Sophie? And Cheryl and Jase?

Worse…how will you face up to yourself?

Despite the stern words, her knees kept knocking and her mouth remained so dry she knew for sure and certain it would be incapable of uttering a sound. The doorman looked across at her for perhaps the twentieth time, and again she avoided eye contact. If she didn't move soon, he might have her arrested for loitering.

A man in a tux came out of the dining area and stopped to say something to the doorman. Security? She didn't think security would wear dinner-suits, but then, what did she know? This was a very high-class venue. The thought

of being thrown out onto the street without a chance of
explaining had her heading for the ladies room. She had
already used it twice. Halfway there, she caught sight of
herself in a huge mirror.

Herself?

What she saw was an elegant blonde wearing moss-
green layered georgette that floated in all kinds of inter-
esting ways in response to her body's undulating motion.
Beneath the softly flowing fabric she saw long, smooth
legs and little sandals that sparkled as they caught the light.
Their high heels were what caused her body to undulate.

As she stopped, absorbed anew by this miracle of Sophie's creation, she noticed the man in the tuxedo eyeing
her again. She recognized that look. He wasn't checking
out a suspicious character—he was checking out the
blonde in the mirror, the woman named Tamara.

Her glossy lips curved into a smile just as her admirer
caught her eye. She gave him an apologetic shrug, tucked
the little evening bag under her arm, and, with a new confidence in her step, she turned toward the doorman.

This was the third time Nick had participated in this
auction. The other times he hadn't minded the attention,
had even played up to the crowd, given them his best smile
and encouraged them to do their worst.

Tonight he simply didn't want to be here.

Get it over with, he thought as he stepped into the spotlight on the small raised dais in front of a well-fed—and
equally well-lubricated—audience. That was all part of the
plan. The more champagne they drank, the more deeply
they dug into their wallets.

Dutifully he responded to the welcoming applause and
the odd wolf whistle, but by the time bidding commenced,
his face ached with the effort of smiling. He supposed he
was out of practice.

Prompted by the celebrity auctioneer's prodding, the bids came helter-skelter, past ten, then twenty, thousand.

"Do I hear twenty-five?"

"You betcha," rang loud and clear from an ancient supporter in the front row, and the crowd roared with delight.

Nick tuned out. *Get it over with*, he repeated silently, *so I can get the hell out of here.* And go where? Back to that cold, hollow apartment, to pace the floorboards well into the morning hours?

He knew the restlessness in his spirit couldn't be fixed as easily as it had in the past. None of the traditional challenges—no mountain, no river, no glacier—could do it. Only Tamara could.

Tamara. He was so lost in thoughts of her, of feeling her in his arms again, that he imagined he heard her voice, raised as if to attract attention.

"I don't think I could have heard you correctly, madam." The auctioneer was peering toward the back of the room. "Would you mind repeating your bid?"

"Five hundred thousand dollars."

He hadn't imagined her voice. She was here, in this room, repeating her killer bid on the last lot. On him.

Nick wasn't the only one stunned. The laughter and chatter subsided to hushed murmurs, accompanied by the swish of fabric and creak of chairs as people turned to stare. Nick stared with them.

"That's a serious bid, madam?" the auctioneer asked.

"Lock the doors so she doesn't escape," a heckler called. The laughter seemed a little strained, expectant, as if the joke might fall flat.

"It's a serious bid, but I can't go any higher."

"In that case…" The auctioneer did his usual *Any more bids? Going once, going twice* patter, before bringing his gavel down. Someone up back started to clap. Gradually the rest of the crowd joined in, the applause rising to a thunderous crescendo that pretty much matched the beating of Nick's heart.

He still couldn't see her, still couldn't be sure he hadn't imagined this whole scenario. Still wasn't sure how he felt about this whole ridiculous scenario.

He stepped off the stage and out of the light...although not out of the spotlight. The auction coordinator had her arm through his, wanting to complete the formalities. Others on the organizing committee gathered around, slapping him on the back and shaking his hand as if he had just performed some amazing act of benevolence.

Some of the crowd were standing, forming an informal guard of honor as they applauded the winning bidder's progress to the front of the room.

And finally he saw her.

T.C. felt her knees start to wobble and was grateful when a woman stepped from the group surrounding Nick to take her arm. That kept her upright. "Well, here she is. Our mystery bidder. I suppose you would like to meet Mr. Corelli?"

"We've met."

His voice sounded as reserved as the first touch of his gaze, and T.C. felt it like a physical blow. What had she expected? Open arms and melting smiles? Maybe not, but a touch of warmth, of encouragement, even of surprise, would have been nice.

The organizer was trying to draw her aside, talking sotto voce of paperwork and the chance of publicity, and T.C. appealed to Nick—to those cool blue eyes.

"Can we handle the formalities later, Yvonne?" he asked.

The woman tutted something about *unknown quantities,* and something definitely unreserved sparked in his eyes. "I can vouch for this lady's check, Yvonne."

"Are you certain?"

"I believe I wrote it myself."

Yvonne's raised eyebrows almost disappeared off her forehead as she added up the score. T.C. felt the weight of a dozen calculating gazes, but there was only one that mattered. It had turned intent, serious, questioning. Her smile was tentative as she held up his check.

"You said if I didn't want it I should give it to charity. I liked the sound of this one."

"It does good work."

"Yes, you do."

Yvonne cleared her throat, and impatience or irritation flickered in Nick's eyes. But he turned to her and smiled. "We will handle the formalities tomorrow. All right?"

But it wasn't a question, not really.

"And could we have a little privacy right now?"

That wasn't a question, either. The group dispersed amid some unsettled muttering, and finally they were alone...alone with a room full of curious onlookers pretending not to watch.

Nick turned his impatient, irritated gaze on her, and T.C. felt her stomach dip. "Now, you want to tell me what this is all about?"

"Well, according to the catalogue, I have bought an adventure weekend with you as my personal guide." She took a deep, nervous gulp of air. "Now, I know it's rather short notice, but I was wondering if you would have this weekend free?"

"You have something in mind?"

She held nothing back when she looked right into his eyes. "I believe I owe you some backstory."

"You needed to come all the way over here, to pay an exorbitant amount of money, to talk to me?"

"I hope it will be worth it."

He gave nothing away in the next moment—a long breath-held moment that meant more to T.C. than any single moment that had ever come before.

Then he gave a swift nod of his head, murmured,

"We'll see what you've got to say, then," and his voice sounded as dark and compelling as the hour before dawn. Then he took her hand and drew her in his wake across the room, through the crowd that parted before them and closed ranks behind them. A crowd that applauded their departure as they would stars leaving the stage.

T.C.'s head was still spinning long after they climbed into the back of a cab and started for whatever address Nick had given.

She felt his gaze on her from across the cab and the distance he seemed to have put between them again. "There were easier ways of doing this, you know."

"I know." She took a deep breath. "But I decided I didn't want to do this the easy way. I decided I should do something right outside that comfort zone."

"Coming to New York wasn't enough?"

"Not to get rid of that check."

"It always comes back to that!"

"Yes, it does, and you want to know why?" She didn't wait for him to say anything, for him to turn any further away from her. "I didn't want Yarra Park or what Joe wanted for us to come between us. I wanted this to be about us, Nick, with no inheritance and no expectations interceding."

Her impassioned plea seemed to fill the enclosed space, to suck up the very air until she felt giddy with lack of oxygen. "Expectations?" he asked slowly.

"Yeah." She smiled, wryly. "Joe wanted us to be together. His wanting you to come over to Australia to tell me about the inheritance, his wanting me to talk you into caring for the place so you would keep it—it was a match-making thing. He wanted us tied together."

He took a long time to digest those words, to turn them over and to formulate his response. And all the while Tamara's heart beat a heady tattoo in her chest.

"And so you wanted to get rid of these ties. You didn't want to be tied to me?"

Here it was. The moment when she put it all on the line. She took a deep breath. "I didn't want to be tied to you by other people or by property. That doesn't mean I didn't want you."

"And you couldn't tell me this before I left Australia?"

"Ridiculous, huh? But I needed to sort it out in my head first, and I needed to take a huge dose of courage, and I needed Cheryl to talk some sense into me."

For the first time he smiled, and it was as if that simple action released an unbearable pressure in her chest. "If she talked you into paying half a million for a weekend with me, then I'm not sure we're talking sense here."

"Oh, I think it might be worth it."

He sobered instantly, and she could feel the intensity of his gaze from across the cab. "You still haven't answered my question. Do you want to be tied to me?"

"I do." She smiled hesitantly. "But only in whatever way you want that to be. I know that I'm difficult, and I know I don't like change, and I know I'm not always courageous."

He stopped her by taking her hand, lifting it to his lips. "It took a whole lot of courage to do what you did tonight, Tamara."

"Maybe, but I'm no prize, and I don't want you to think you owe me anything."

This time he stopped her by kissing her lips.

"Will you stop prevaricating and get to the point? Do you love me? Is that what you are trying to say? Because that sure as hell is all I want to hear from you, sweet lips."

But the look in his eyes gave the lie to the frustration in his words. They were smiling and offering exactly the right dose of encouragement. They invited her; they coaxed her; they gave her courage.

"I love you, Nick, but that doesn't mean you have to—"

"I love you, okay? Now will you stop trying to let me off the hook?" His touched a gentle finger to her lips. "You're what I've been searching for."

"The ultimate challenge?" she asked wryly.

He laughed, the sound low and sweet and jammed full of his feelings for her. "Well, sweetheart, I figure you are looking like one hell of a lifetime challenge." Then his eyes turned serious. "But I meant I'd been searching for the place I belonged. You are that place, Tamara. You are my home. I love you, green eyes."

Tears pooled in those eyes and spilled over, sliding down her cheeks as Nick took her mouth, as he kissed her in the way only he knew how, and she didn't bother hiding them. She let them fall as she kissed him back, as she touched his cheeks, his hair, as she breathed against his lips, "Welcome home, Niccolo."

* * * * *

INTIMATE MOMENTS™

is proud to present

Romancing the Crown

*With the help of their powerful allies,
the royal family of Montebello is determined
to find their missing heir. But the search for the
beloved prince is not without danger—or passion!*

**This exciting twelve-book series begins in January and
continues throughout the year with these fabulous titles:**

Available at your favorite retail outlet.

Silhouette®
Where love comes alive™